Splitting

Also by Mario Milosevic

15 Strange Tales of Crime and Mystery
Animal Life
Claypot Dreamstance
The Coma Monologues
The Doctor and the Clown
Entangled Realities (with Kim Antieau)
Fantasy Life
Kyle's War
The Last Giant
Labor Days
Love Life
Miniatures
Terrastina and Mazolli: a Novel in 99-word Episodes

Splitting

Mario Milosevic

Green Snake
PUBLISHING

Splitting
by Mario Milosevic

Copyright © 2017 by Mario Milosevic

mariowrites.com

ISBN-13: 978-1-949644-11-1

Cover image © Adam Tinney | Dreamstime.com

Thanks to Nancy Milosevic
Thanks to Michael Brantley

Published by Green Snake Publishing
www.greensnakepublishing.com

*A multiple personality
is in a certain sense normal.*

George H. Mead

It's a different world today (isn't it always?) and it takes some effort to remember my early days in Northern Ontario in the mid and late 50s, now, astonishingly, part of another century. We, that is, my parents and I, lived in Valton, a small town in the Northern Ontario woods, named after the uranium mining company that built it and stocked it with miners and their families.

I use the term stock deliberately. There was nothing humane about the way the mine brought in workers or the way they treated them once they had them. The company's operation consisted of two shafts sunk into the rocks only a few miles from the town. My father worked there, bringing up the uranium ore that would give him a killing cancer thirty years later. Not that anyone, least of all I, could prove it, but sometimes you don't need proof. You just know. I used to tell my students it wasn't enough to know the result of a theorem, you also had to be able to prove it. It was the most basic practice of doing math, so I don't expect you to believe me when I tell you that working the Valton mine killed my father. Just understand that I consider it equivalent to a mathematical axiom: an unshakeable belief that withstands any attempt to cast doubt upon it.

I suppose people were aware of the possible adverse effects of handling uranium ore back then, but it wasn't effectively communicated to the miners. The shafts and tunnels of the mine were saturated with radon gas, which the miners had rustled up out of the rocks with their drilling and blasting and general mucking about in the ground. That radon attached itself to dust particles which the miners inhaled.

Today mining operations are much more conscious of safety, but in the time I'm talking about, the time of my youth, the innocent time for me and the world, radon was on no one's list of safety concerns.

I'll put it this way: Valton Mines had no difficulty finding laborers willing to dig up uranium. In fact, uranium mining was considered safer than coal mining since it was a hard rock. My father considered it a godsend that he didn't have to work a coal mine. And uranium was the raw material for the promised nuclear revolution: clean and abundant cheap energy for all. The cold war was cranking up into full gear. Canada was only too willing to provide the uranium that the United States was only too willing to buy in order to fuel their nuclear submarines and commercial reactors of the times.

I don't suppose anyone knows exactly why people return to

the places of their younger days, except to relive the time when everything was in the future, all of life was potential, not dissipated possibility, and the whole enterprise seemed capable of affording some sense of meaning. Not that I've had a bad life. And it's not over, by any means, but more than half of it is gone, which gives one's daily routine a kind of melancholy tinge. It gave me the impetus to take stock, as a way of orienting myself back in the water, preparatory to continuing the course set for me so long ago.

I've retired from a professorship in a small community college where I taught mathematics for many years. Math was an early passion of mine, but as the years went by, I lost interest in it and the truth is I was never exceptionally good at it. My students, for the most part, did not move me to rekindle my interest, and in the last decade or so, I was mostly going through the motions. It was about that time that I began to seek out events from my past, and, most specifically, the time I split my being into two.

That sounds like an odd thing to say, like I was an atom in a nuclear fission reaction, and I don't expect you to take such a statement at face value. Let me recount my story, as best I can remember it, and I'll let you decide for yourself if I'm telling the truth or merely allowing myself to be deluded by a seductive untruth.

The time I'm thinking of was soon after my sister died. She was only a week or so old, born with ghastly birth defects. She had never even come home from the company-built clinic and I had never seen her. Only knew of her condition from overheard and whispered conversations between my parents. We had buried her only a few days before the events I will describe here, and that fact colored much of my actions. I was in grief over the effect it had on my parents, the way they seemed to embrace sadness and dejection. The way they changed so quickly into depressed people. How could such a thing happen, and what did it mean for me? Was I going to be abandoned by them so they could nurture their new-found melancholy with all due zeal and determination?

Such are the thoughts of a kid at such times. I was really grieving the possibility that I might become emotionally orphaned and, being just a kid, hardly knew what grief was and certainly had no skills to cope with the possibility. I knew only that I was under threat. I can imagine, just possibly, other nine-year-olds being more cognizant and sympathetic to other people's pain, but I was not such a one.

I do recall that my sister, tucked away in the cemetery just up the road from Valton, was constantly on my mind. The thought that she could die made me realize I could die, and there is likely no more sobering thought for anyone, much less me. I may not have been a normal nine year old boy, but I'm not sure. Do nine-year-olds generally brood about their future? Or concern themselves with when and how they will die? Probably not, but I did.

The woods that once stood where the cemetery was had been pushed back to allow room for the graves. That's how Valton, the mining company, did things: no finesse or respect for the land. Bring in the bulldozers to knock over the trees, then scrape the soil smooth with earth movers and do what had to be done. Or what they thought had to be done for the sake of their operations.

There weren't all that many graves in the cemetery since the town was still new, only about 12 years old, and most of the families were young. But even such a town as Valton will have its deaths. A young mother among them. Someone's grandfather. A couple of miners that died in a cave-in. And my sister.

I don't know what my parents thought about having their daughter buried there. It was nothing like what a real cemetery should look like. Even I, kid that I was, saw that. The grass was weedy and overgrown. The surrounding land was nothing much to look at or experience, just a tangle of uprooted logs piled up like toys on the edge of the clearing.

I could see the cemetery from a similar pile pushed up at the edge of town. We called that pile the tangle, an unruly mess of old logs at the east edge of Valton. That pile was left over from when they cleared land for the town. I'm a long way from the tangle and Valton now. I was born in Valton, still consider it my home, as sub-standard as it was, and I still think of my sister who I never knew. She seems to live in my heart even now. How does that happen? It scarcely seems possible. How does a person keep the memory of someone who burned only flickeringly and only for a brief time? It's a mystery, like many mysteries, with no real answer that makes any sense.

And how can I adequately describe Valton? It's gone now, a victim of the end of the cold war. Uranium demand dropped and Valton, like other mines, ceased operations. The village where I grew up turned into a ghost town. We were long scattered by then, one of the first families to leave. I had gone away to university in Toronto, and my father had found a job with the railroad in Winnipeg, Manitoba, where he and my mother moved, and where my mother still lives, enduring winters born out of some mutant arctic dream. My father's been gone more than ten years now and I do believe my mother uses those awful winters to try to freeze the sorrow out of her. She tells me how the cold brings her comfort. It pushes her inward, physically and emotionally, keeping her inside with the doors and windows secured against the freezing winds and giving her comfort. The same way my father found comfort underground, the whole world around him like a cocoon.

But all of that, our leaving and the woods beginning to reclaim the site, came later. When we lived there we, or at least I, hardly knew of anything else in the world. Valton was my realm and it was the very definition of remote. It sat in a bulldozed clearing in Northern Ontario, some 80 miles off the Trans-Canada Highway, on the end of a narrow two lane road that deteriorated into gravel and dirt for miles at a time. Valton's chief point of interest, for a kid, was the tangle. Kids my age and younger would climb all over it and crawl down between the rotting logs, some covered with moss and fungi, into the interior of the tangle. A welcoming darkness, eerie, comforting, and dangerous all at the same time, held the interior of the tangle in its soft clutches. It was cool in the summer and in the winter, frost-trimmed and slick with ice and snow, it offered an even more dangerous and inviting refuge. I liked the thought of its malevolence, like a treacherous treehouse calling to me.

Creatures lived down there: rats and raccoons. I'd hear them scampering away as I approached. Probably other animals, too. We peeled off hunks of old bark to reveal swarming ant colonies. We pressed our fingers into the wood, soft and mushy in some places, but still strong and resilient in others. The tangle was the best playground ever for the kids of Valton. The mining company had built a small park with swings and monkey bars in town, but no kid spent much time there. Not when the tangle's dangerous layers called to us like a siren.

The most vivid memories I have of the tangle involve the times I would sit up on top of the pile, all the crisscrossing branches beneath me, stretched down to the ground in a snarl of twisted limbs. Sometimes, thinking about descending into the morass of wood, made my blood rush. Other times, I would be so frightened of the possibility of my own demise that I could hardly even consider dropping into it. At those times I imagined a more daring version of myself, like a super hero mutant, gripping the branches like a monkey and dropping into the entanglement.

I offer this memory as a way of explaining my ambivalence about the tangle. It was inviting but also repelling. The danger in the tangle may have been exaggerated. It's hard to say. I recall some bumps and bruises among my peers, but nothing really awful. No broken bones or concussions. Nothing like that. Certainly no deaths. The variety of injury was exactly congruent with what one might expect from more conventional playground apparatus.

The mothers in town would worry about us and swat us about the ears for daring to put ourselves in such danger when we returned with scrapes and bumps after time spent in the tangle. The pile could shift at any time and crush us under the weight of all that wood. Or so our mothers thought. In reality, such things seldom happened. The tangle had pretty much settled into a sound structure by the time I was spending my hours there.

In any case, we didn't care. We hoped the logs could shift and threaten to kill us. That danger was better than regular life in Valton. The forest always seemed like it was encroaching on the town, ready to take back what Valton Mines had yanked away so unceremoniously. I had the uncanny feeling that the forest was patiently waiting for us to leave. Then it would slowly fill in the hole we had made in its expanse and erase any evidence that any of us had been there. The place where I was born was only borrowed from the wild. I had the notion of leaving part of myself there, in the tangle, as a monument of sorts.

Maybe I did.

My mother begged my father to ask the mine to do something about the tangle. Bury it, take it away, burn it. Anything. But my father would hear none of it. He said it didn't pay to be a troublemaker so we just had to put up with the tangle, and then he told me to stay away from it. I thought I saw him wink as he said it, but couldn't be sure. In any case, both of us, my father and I, knew I wasn't going to stop climbing the tangle.

My mother sighed and muttered something about going to the mine bosses herself. This turned my father's face red and he slammed his fist down on the table and told her she was not to do any such thing.

I remember that battle between them with great clarity. My father was deathly afraid of being perceived as a nuisance and my mother was deathly afraid of me getting injured or killed. I didn't know what to think. Kids climbed things. There was no mystery there: it was going to happen. If some of us got cut or bruised, so be it. It was no big deal.

To get to the mine itself, you had to go a further three or four miles from the town, north past the tangle, up an even more primitive road than the one that connected Valton to the main highway. That road wound through deciduous woods, past rocky escarpments, and over mossy hills. A spur of railroad track looped around the town on the other side and terminated at the mine's mill. Rocks came up from underground on conveyer belts which emptied into silos at the mill where giant steel jaws crushed the raw ore into tons of rubble. The tracks took boxcars of the crushed ore from the mine to some smelting operation elsewhere that none of us knew or cared about. That was some other town's concern, not ours.

The mine operated all year round, in sweltering summers and bone-brittling winters. Underground it was always the same: slightly humid and comfortably warm. At least, that's what my father reported. We envied him his artificial comfort when we had to deal with the extremes of the natural world up on the surface.

My parents were immigrants from Hungary. They had come to Canada looking for stability and prosperity. No one told them, before they came, that they could have those things only if they worked back-breaking and soul-killing jobs like mining ore.

My father worked three shifts: one week from eight in the morning to four in the afternoon, the next week from four in the afternoon to midnight, and the week after that from midnight to eight in the morning. His schedule rotated endlessly through these three shifts which were supposed to be fair to all the workers, but which only served to keep them all permanently fatigued. Just when he got used to one shift, they put him on another. My father became a kind of ghost presence in my life. I never knew when he would be gone, or when we had to be quiet in the middle of day so as not to disturb his sleep.

The whole town was like that, with all the miners working those crazy swing shifts. We were mostly a very quiet community, tiptoeing around with subdued voices. Even the children. People got cabin fever way more than was healthy for them and they would see things: lights in the sky, floating somethings filling the air over distant swamps. Wildlife, mostly bear and moose, moving like shadows everywhere. Deer and elk as well. Occasionally a wild cat. We often didn't know if they were real or not, but sometimes it was obvious because these big creatures would wander into town. Guys with firearms would be very happy to take them down with a rifle shot or two. On those occasions no one cared about the noise. The mothers, especially, were concerned that wild creatures might harm their children.

In any case, no one in town had much sympathy for the animals. If they were stupid enough to root around in our garbage, they were stupid enough to dispatch without scruple. Or so the sentiment seemed to be.

Insects, too, plagued our existence. Especially mosquitoes, which invaded Valton every year in swarms of misery that made us all cranky. Valton Mines brought in foggers that dispersed clouds of insecticide into the air and our lungs. We didn't care about what it was doing to us, we were only too glad to have the mosquitoes killed.

My mother devoted her life to me and my father. She kept an immaculate house and cooked three meals a day without fail and without complaint. At least, that's what I thought then. Now I think how wretched her existence must have been, stuck in the woods with few friends and hardly anything in the way of a social life. She must have longed for her days in Hungary, a place that was at least part of her being. She must have felt like an eternal stranger in Canada.

The families who lived in Valton were mostly immigrants, willing to do the dangerous work of pulling ore from the ground in the middle of nowhere. Barely five hundred people called the town home. Everyone lived in company-made houses. For many, it was a material, if not a spiritual, step up from what they were used to. We had families from Poland, Serbia, Italy, and Hungary. Probably more that I don't remember. They were mostly refugees from poor rural existences. My parents didn't talk much about Hungary. That was all in the past. Actually, it seemed none of their previous lives meant much to the residents of Valton. I never knew if it was because their old lives were miserable, or that their old lives were actually better, and they didn't want to think about what they had left behind for life in Valton. We were all Canadians, that was all that seemed to matter. All the adults spoke broken English, some more broken than others. Many of the kids were fluently bilingual, speaking their parent's language at home, and speaking Canadian English in school and with our peers. A lot of us remarked on this double existence. Even though our parents didn't want to talk about their homelands, they still spoke in the language of their homelands. I knew Hungarian and spoke it with my parents, but that knowledge is long gone now, part of my old life.

The only store in Valton was company-owned and run. My parents complained that their prices were twice what they should have been and often threatened to leave town to do their shopping, but that was impractical on a regular basis. People had cars, and they would take road trips out of town, but those were few and far between. Once you got on the Trans-Canada, it was still another hundred miles or so to any city you would want to visit.

I went to school, of course, as sanctioned by provincial law. That, at least, was not company-run or owned, but it was not exactly state of the art, either. The school building was a converted prefab barn. All grades, from kindergarten to high school senior, were crammed into it. The classrooms ringed the perimeter of the barn. We felt like we were kept in stalls, like livestock, waiting for the teacher to bring us her lessons like a farmer shoveling out feed to his animals. The barn was cold in the winter and hot in late spring, which is approximately the time I want to tell you about now.

There were just two of us, my friend and me, both of us nine years old and trying to speed up a boring Saturday afternoon by spending time at the edge of a pond situated next to a berm of gravel and dirt which supported the railroad tracks some twenty-five feet or so above us. An abundance of trees held up a canopy of what seemed like millions of leaves over us, so vibrant and trembling with life that it seemed they were as eager as we were to shake off the winter blahs.

We nursed a certain ennui, vague and unfamiliar, thinking about having to go back to school in two days. My weariness was accentuated by the recent death of my sister. It still seemed unfair. First that her life was so wretched, then that it was so short. Under those circumstances, with the precarious nature of living made so abundantly clear to me, what could school possibly matter?

But at the same time, what did this Saturday, like every other Saturday, matter? We lived in Valton, after all. It was the first warm day of the year, which got us outside, but didn't exactly fill us with unbounded joy.

We were free range kids. Our parents let us out of our houses and expected that we would be gone all day, playing games with other kids, or roaming the woods that surrounded the town on all sides. Such things did occur, but not always. Often the two of us were lone roamers, walking around on our own for hours at a time, endlessly circling Valton in the woods, or just kicking around town, aimless, or climbing around the tangle. We walked over outcroppings of rocks and were told in no uncertain terms that if we saw a wild creature like a bear or moose, we were to turn around immediately and return home. For all other eventualities, we were to stay outside.

The pond we frequented called to us for reasons we neither understood, nor cared to investigate. There was something pre-ternatural about the bright green rim of algae, like a watermelon rind, that circled the pond with almost geometric exactitude, wavering from its half-foot width by only an inch or so at every point. The water was clear and clean and the pond was teeming with tadpoles, each frenzied black blob like a shimmering ink drop flowing through the water and trailing a flipping-flapping wake of tail.

They're just trapped in this pond, I said.

So what? said my friend.

It'd be awful to live like that. Stuck in one place.

My friend laughed. We live like that, he said. We're stuck in Valton. You should feel sorry for us.

I didn't think I should feel sorry for anyone, even though I felt sorry for myself for what was happening to my family in the wake of my sister's death. It seemed the most precarious thing, the bonds of relationship. My well-being depended upon those bonds staying whole, and their wholeness was completely out of my power.

Anyway, I was just making an observation, but my friend had a point. Our world was just as small as the world of the tad-poles.

I have sometimes wondered, in my idle times between grading student papers, what exactly it was about those tad-poles that generated such interest in us. We loved to watch them swimming around endlessly, as though they were trying to paint black trails of ink in the water. Today, from the perspective of half a century, it feels like they had some kind of second life, composed not of individual blobs, but of the accumulation of blobs. They were an entity unto themselves, and our removal of a few of them was not going to destroy the whole, but merely give the whole a slight injury. An injury that would quickly be repaired as the remaining tadpoles moved to fill in the void.

We dipped a jar into the pond, waited for a few of the tadpoles to swim into it, then raised it out of the pond and clamped a lid on the top. We held the jar up to see the tadpoles swimming in aimless circles behind the curved glass. We swished the water around some, just to get the tadpoles going with more agitation.

Don't we have to punch holes in the lid so they can breathe? I asked my friend.

He shrugged. I don't know. Don't they breathe the water?

Frogs don't breathe water.

These aren't frogs. Yet.

If someone asked us what we were going to do with the tadpoles I don't think we would have had a coherent answer. Collecting tadpoles was just something you did at that age. You took them home and you kept them in the jar and the next day you might take them back to the pond, or they might die. We didn't know which would happen and part of being a kid was letting the process take its course so we could see what would happen. It was our primitive version of the scientific method.

Now, of course, looking back, it seems like a cruel thing to have done, but to us, in those days, it was only a part of being who we were.

We held the jar up higher, so it caught the rays of the sun. We shielded our eyes from the glinting sparkles on the surface of the jar. Behind us, high up on the tracks, a kid's voice, older than us by a couple of years, flowed over the rocks of the berm and snagged itself on our ears.

Hey. What you doing down there?

It was a voice I recognized from school. A kid a few grades beyond ours, someone new to Valton. His father was a big mucky muck at the mine, one of the bosses. This kid had a way about him that warned people off, like he was going to get nasty, maybe violent, at any second. Not that I understood any of that then. I only knew he was menacing, and his danger was mysterious because he didn't actually do anything physically intimidating. It was all attitude. I knew where he lived. His company-built house was a little bigger that our company-built house. If Valton had a wrong and right side of the tracks, he would have been from right side, except that by any objective measure all of Valton was clearly on the wrong side of the tracks.

I started to answer him but my friend grabbed my arm and said Shut up. He used a voice I hadn't heard from him before, as though he had taken someone else's words for his own.

I shut up without another sound.

My friend leaned close to me. He just wants to get us riled up, he said.

The boy at the track called down to us again. Hey faggots, he said. I asked you what you were doing down there.

Come on, said my friend. Let's go. He picked up the jar of tadpoles and we started walking away from the pond and away from the kid tossing insults our way.

We took a few steps, then an explosion of broken glass burst the air around us. My friend jumped. The jar's lid remained in his hand, gripped by his fingertips, but the jar with the tadpoles had completely shattered. Wriggling black globes writhed on the ground between shards of glass. I looked up at the other guy, who stood with his hands on his hips, grinning with self-assured smugness. I had to admit, that was a pretty good shot.

He threw a rock at us, I said.

He's going to throw more, said my friend. Let's get out of here.

We took another few steps. My friend bent down and covered his head with his hands. I thought he was being ridiculous. The guy wasn't going to hit us with a rock. Was he?

I looked up and saw him hefting a good-sized stone. He put his hand back behind his head and released the rock with a strong motion, like he was pitching a baseball. My friend was still safely bent over, his head tucked under his arms, but I, too curious to see what was happening, too interested in the out-come, didn't turn my gaze from the rock as it grew rapidly bigger until it almost filled my view. For a moment, my perception of events twisted on itself and I felt like I was being pushed on a rail directly toward it. Inexplicably, an image of my sister's grave came to mind: a small headstone, the fresh ground heaped up next to it. My parents and me standing in front of it. I had my hands in their hands. I wanted to pull away, but understood the moment was theirs, not mine, and so I remained completely still while they wept for their child.

That was the stance I adopted as the rock came toward me. I was completely still, as though observing the stone's flight with a melancholy reverence. And then it was too late to turn away and the rock—flat, sharp-edged, and spinning—smacked into my skull just above my eye. I felt immediate pain and a jolt of nausea, like someone had punched me in the stomach. The stone broke the skin above my eye and released a torrent of blood that flowed over my eyebrows and dripped onto my eye-ball and down my face to my shirt, impossibly white next to the round bloodstains blooming on it.

I thought of my sister, again, newly demised and folded back into the ground. She barely had a chance to experience the world. The world barely had a chance to torture her. She was born tortured, and did not survive long. The blood that ran through her veins hardly had a chance to become acclimated to the cycle before the whole apparatus came to a halt. I imag-ined her almost like a clockwork mechanism, damaged by some fall, clunking along for a while, then toppling with big Xs on her eyes. All these things erupted into my brain when I saw my own blood. Mysterious things: blood and death and my sister.

When the boy on the track saw that he had connected, he looked startled and immediately turned and ran. To where, I can't say for sure, but it appeared that he was going back to town. To confess his crime? Surely not. Maybe to hide out, perhaps establish an alibi that he could use should I ever accuse him of his assault.

My friend groaned. What the fuck? he said. He sounded scared. More scared than I thought was warranted, especially in his use of what my mother called miner's language. I could only guess that he was not familiar with the sight of blood.

The wound stung and I felt a persistent wooziness, like I was going to fall over, but I managed to stay upright. I'm not sure how. It felt like some other person was holding me up, laboring to keep my feet steady and unwobbly.

I tried to stop the gushing flow by putting my hand over the wound, but to little effect. I didn't know then that head wounds often bleed profusely. My thoughts were confused and jumbled. The world looked like it was vibrating, and a buzzing noise enveloped me. Such strange sensations, like the world was about to split open. I was disoriented, but I did have a definite sense that all that blood couldn't be a good thing to be losing.

Did I think I was going to die? It's hard to say now. When you're nine years old, you don't even know what death is, not really. You think you do when your week-old sister dies, but it's really nothing more than a complete mystery. Even today, decades after those times, I'm still not sure what death is.

So even if I did think I was going to bleed to death, the experience of it was not necessarily a frightening thing to me. I mostly didn't like the slippery feeling of the blood. It was unpleasant and it was making a mess of my shirt.

I need to get home, I said to my friend. My voice sounded weak, even to me. I began walking up the slope of the tracks, but had to bend down to make my way over the rocks. As I did so, I felt a pressure in my head. It was like gallons of blood wanted to escape the confines of my skull and get out. I knew my skull wasn't going to crack open, but that's exactly what it felt like it was trying to do, and that started getting me as scared as my friend. I felt a tingle of fear through my whole body, like I was going to spin out of control and tear my being apart.

Where'd that guy go? I said.

I don't know, said my friend. Jesus. Are you going to be okay? What should we do?

We don't have to do anything, I said. I just need to get home.

Your Mom's going to be mad.

It was true. Maybe not as mad as the time I shit my pants because I didn't get home in time, but pretty mad. I wasn't sure how my father would react. He was at work. Probably wouldn't get home until I was all bandaged up. He might actually think it was a good thing that I got wounded. I think I remember that I had noticed that some older guys liked the thought of getting into a fight. It was one of those things I wondered if maybe all older males enjoyed, but some of them kept that fact to themselves. Only a few let on, so it was this big secret that everyone knew, but that the adults thought children didn't know.

Or maybe, to put it more clearly, it was one of the things they kept from us, but that we understood only partially and would learn about in more detail when we got older. Someone, probably my mother, maybe my father, would sit down with me and go over a list of things that any adult had to know. Things like what kind of clothes to wear, how to behave in all possible situations, and how to fix things. Whether I should get married, what kind of job I should get, and where I should live. I was convinced there was a right way to do everything, but to find out what the right way was, I needed help. Everyone needed help. I was sure all those things were probably in some book somewhere and when the time was right, every kid got a copy.

I never thought to look for it, though, just assumed it would appear for me at the magical moment when it would be most useful.

I continued to crawl up the hill, to get up to the tracks and over them, then down to our house. It was very slow going, though, and the rocks had an unfamiliar feel to them, like they were made of felt. I kept thinking about that book. The knowledge it contained. I wondered if it was right that all that information was kept from kids. Kids knew so little about the world that it might be a good idea to get that information early on rather than later. But then it occurred to me that maybe kids weren't ready for all that knowledge. Maybe kids needed to be kept ignorant for their own good. I didn't like that thought, but it might possibly make some kind of sense. Probably the book explained it.

While I had been considering the book, I kept climbing. I thought if I wasn't careful, my feet might slip between the rocks and fall into the ground. I wouldn't know what to do then. The ground might grab me up and hold me, like a dog biting onto someone's leg and not letting go. The thought didn't disturb me. I found it fascinating to think the ground could do that.

I was the kind of kid that thought those thoughts and didn't let them worry me, but on that day I did feel some anxiety. I wondered if my blood loss was making my brain go in dangerous directions. I mean, there was no way the ground was going to grab onto me. It didn't have teeth and jaws, right? Right?

Then my thoughts returned to my wound. The gash above my eye, still spilling blood. I reviewed how I got it, the event barely two or three minutes old, but already part of history, not experience. The image of the rock coming down the berm already felt like a dream.

I wondered if when I explained what happened I could present it as a fight. It wasn't a fight, not really, but my wound was the kind I might get from a fight, so I was pretty sure that counted. When it healed and scarred over, anyone would believe I got it in a fight. A real fight. It seemed to me, at that moment, that I could use the fake fight thing to my advantage. Maybe get others to be scared of me. I always wanted people to fear me, but I was not the sort of kid who was accorded that kind of respect. I was usually the ignored or picked-on kid.

My mother was going to feel sorry for me when she saw the gash. I was pretty sure of that. Sorry and mad at the same time. After all, I was cut pretty bad. I was sure she was not going to like that my white shirt was all bloody. The shirt was my idea. I insisted on getting a pure white shirt. I liked the color. They had a good stock of them at the company store, but they weren't selling many. No one wanted a white shirt. Except me. My mother wanted something else for me, but I talked her into my choice. It was maybe the first time that I ever really asserted a preference without a whine backing it up. I merely told her that I liked the white shirt and wanted to wear it. She said it would show stains and I said that was okay, other people wore white shirts, important people, and they didn't worry about stains. And when I said that she got this look like she didn't exactly know who she was talking to and I wanted to tell her that it was me, it was her son, and maybe I had just gotten a hold of one of the pages of the book. That's what it felt like. That some insight from the book had come to me like a miracle.

But I didn't tell her that. Not there in the store. She let me get the white shirt. I put it on proudly and wore it to school and didn't care about the strange looks I got from my classmates. My friend said he liked the shirt. He even asked me where I got it. I told him it was at the company store and he whistled, like nothing nice looking could come from there. But it did.

My friend had his hand on my shoulder. He looked scared. More scared than I felt. Come on, he said. Get up. You passed out.

What? I looked around. I was on my back. Strands of some grassy weed that snaked up from between the rocks tickled my ear. I brushed it away, but it didn't work. The blade just seemed to want to move into my ear.

You gotta get up, said my friend. Come on.

I didn't want to get up. I just wanted to stay on the ground. I put my hand up to the spot above my eye. I touched cloth. What's this?

I wrapped my sock around your head, said my friend. To stop the bleeding.

Your sock? Gross! I went to pull it off, but he grabbed my arm and stopped me.

Fuck, man, said my friend. Don't mess with that. It's keeping you from bleeding.

But your sock! I said.

He gripped my arm tighter, like he wanted to break it. You're all fucked up, he said. Stop being an air head and stand up and walk. You need to get home. Fuck!

I let my head settle back on the rocks and I looked up at the sky. White clouds moved across my field of vision. They made me think of my shirt. My stupid white shirt. I propped myself up on my elbows.

I think I'm going to puke, I said.

Jesus Christ! said my friend. Stop this shit and get it fucking together. I don't want you dying on me.

I laughed. I'm not going to die, I said. I just feel like puking is all.

A shadow loomed up behind me. At the same time, I heard the distant rumble, almost a trembling in the rocks more than a sound, that indicated a train was on its way.

What's this? The rock thrower's voice behind me.

Fuck, whispered my friend.

Taking care of your buddy? the strange voice again.

I twisted my head around. Hey, I said. You're the guy who threw the rock at me.

Rock? I don't know about any rock. The guy bent down and grabbed my shirt and pulled me up so my eyes were more or less level with his. I think you ran into something, he said. Isn't that what happened? He put his knee in my belly and pushed hard on it so my stomach felt like I was going to split in two, like a bag tearing open.

Hey, said my friend. Can't you see he's hurt?

I see he has your sock on his head. What's that? Some kind of faggot thing?

Then he dragged me up a few yards until we were beside the tracks. Hear that? he said.

I listened. It was like an earthquake was getting ready to split the ground. It wasn't so much an event, as the promise of an event. The train was coming. I felt the trembling on the ground. A long whistle seeped in through the sock and my skull until it got to my ears. Or brain. Something. I was losing the sense of being somewhere and starting to feel like I was in this limbo between reality and fantasy.

That's your death, said the kid who threw the rock at me. Death on a train, ha ha. Gonna fucking cut your head off. He pulled me up and over the near track, so my neck lay on the rail. The metal was smooth and polished, clean as a washed pan. My head pounded from the pain. Blood began oozing out from under my friend's sock. My cheek brushed against the wooden tie. I saw red splotches fill my field of vision, like my blood was covering my eyeball.

I could leave you here, said the guy.

What'd I do to you? I said, barely able to get the words out. They felt like soft marbles in my mouth. Or maybe tadpoles squirming free of my teeth and tongue.

He laughed. Do? Fuck. You don't have to do anything except fucking die. Like those fucking frog things in your jar. They're going to die. Just like you.

The sound of the train came through the track, like the track was a speaker. It crawled up through my neck and went into my skull, adding to the machinations that were turning my head into an unfamiliar collection of bits and pieces. The shards of awareness felt like they might have been my head, once, but now they were a collection of more or less unrelated chunks of material that reached for some semblance of cohesion. The rumble of the tracks threatened to shake that tentative cohesion loose. I pushed against the boy's arms, trying to gain some purchase against him, but I was like a minnow in his hands. He laughed.

You think you can fight me?

I didn't answer, but I didn't have to. He sat back on the rocks next to the rail, as if he planned to be there for some time. He didn't release his pressure on me, though, and I pushed some more but to no avail. I tried moving my arms around to grab him or push his elbows away, but there, too, the angle was wrong and I could get no purchase on him. When I tried to twist my head around, I saw his smug expression out of the corner of my eye. He was all self-satisfied and relaxed. I was no threat or danger to him at all.

It did occur to me that he couldn't hold me down until the train arrived because then he would be killed too. But he might possibly be able to release me at the last possible instant and I would not be able to get away. Or maybe he was a crazy kid who wanted to die and he wanted to take me with him. I wanted to have the book right then. I needed the parts of it that would tell me how to deal with this completely unreasonable person.

Then, abruptly, the smug expression floated away and he looked first startled, then pained, and slid out of my field of view.

The pressure on my cheek and neck released. The bulb of my head, floating on the stem of my neck, felt like a helium-filled balloon suddenly released to the air. I lifted my skull from the track in time to see the guy fall over across some ties. The train, which I thought was still a long way off, loomed large in front of me and wailed its horn into the air with a long blaring blast. The sound of it. Hurt my head. As if I didn't know the train was there. Didn't the guy driving the train see that I could see him? What was wrong with him, making his horn rip my body apart?

I was not in any shape to estimate the time remaining to us, my tormentor and me, but it probably wasn't much more than about ten seconds.

My friend stood over the guy. He breathed in big gulps of air and seemed to choke on them. A good-sized rock, maybe ten pounds or so, lay next to the fallen kid, between the tracks. I saw that my friend must have dropped it on the boy's head. I wasn't even sure if the boy was alive or dead, but I said: We have to drag him off the tracks.

Fuck him, said my friend. Let him die. He was going to kill you. He grabbed at my arm to try to pull me away from the tracks.

The wheels of the train began a piercing squeal that seemed to make all my cells tremble in sympathy, as though each of them was a bell and they had all been set ringing at the same time.

No, no, I said. We can't just let him get rolled over. I was sure my friend didn't hear me. I bent down and wrapped my hand around the older kid's wrist. He felt warm but lifeless. A queasy shot of something foreign—so many new and upsetting things in the last few minutes—coursed through my system. Systems.

Grab his other arm, I said.

But my friend stepped away from the tracks and folded his arms in front of him.

The train.

The train wasn't stopping. Couldn't stop.

COME ON! I screamed. Grab his other arm.

My friend shook his head. No.

I bent down and took the guy's other hand and brought them together and pulled up and out. My feet skidded on the loose rocks next to the track and his head hit the track, but I didn't care that much. Whatever damage he got from the rail was at least what was coming to him. Anyway, there wasn't time to care. I dragged the rest of him over the track. His hips hit the rail. I thought I heard something break, but, really, there was no way to hear anything except the train's horn and wheels and engine, so I might have imagined it.

I pulled hard and moved my feet in a backwards shuffle until his legs cleared the rail with barely a second or two to spare. The train blurred past me with unreasonable speed and soul-shattering noise. The vibrations penetrated into my chest cavity, my throat, and my wound. I gulped breaths and stood over the guy. I saved him. My would-be killer.

The insistent bulk of the train, all that metal, filled the world. Each box car was a beat in a drum solo the train executed on the rails, punctuated by the screech of the wheels.

My friend was on the other side. I saw his feet through the under carriage of the train. He bounced from side to side like a pinball. With the train between us, separating our worlds, it felt like something bigger had happened. Our disagreement was more than a friendly difference of opinion, it was a fundamental difference in how we viewed the world and our role in it. It was the kind of thing that friendships turn and end on. I wouldn't have put it in those words at that time, but I still felt the illusion of our bond slip into nothing.

The train was so loud. I wanted it to stop. It made my head wound hurt even more, the way it pushed blood through my veins. The guy at my feet stirred. He moved his legs in a scrambling motion, as though attempting to crawl away. Or was he trying to stand up? I couldn't tell, but having saved his life, I felt I was owed a little something, so I kicked him, hard, in the ribs. He doubled over on himself. He held his chest. Blood dripped from my wound. It coursed down my check to the end of my mouth. I stuck out my tongue and caught some of the flow on the tip. I was so thirsty.

I wanted to hit the guy often and hard. The impulse felt real and true, like I was meant to do damage to him. I kicked him twice more. Once on his hands, and then once in his thighs. It crossed my mind to kick him in the crotch, but I refrained. That seemed too intimate.

I stood over him and pondered the notion of justice. Had I avenged my wound? Did I give as good as I got? I wasn't sure, but it felt approximately right, and at that moment I didn't have anything else to go on except my gut feeling. I had an urge to do more, maybe try to break his knees, or push his face into the rocks.

Whatever need I had for damaging this strangely violent kid simply evaporated and I let it slip away. It was replaced by a melancholy feeling that overtook me with a heaviness and weight I hardly recognized. It was like boredom magnified a million times. It felt as though someone had lifted the biggest backpack onto my shoulders and filled it with all that rock that had been pulled out of Valton mine. I still wanted to hurt the kid, but could not muster the energy necessary to continue hurting him. It was probably the first inkling I had in my life that desires were sometimes destructive.

And I also had the uncanny notion that it wasn't me doing the damage. It was some mutant copy of me. I thought that if I wanted to, I could step out of myself and watch myself attacking the rock thrower.

I looked back at the train. I was only a few feet from it. The box cars flashed by, train logos and graffiti punctuating the air with staccato rhythm. Each car held tons of ore. My father hacked some of that ore from the ground. I saw my friend's legs, the bottoms of them, on the other side of the train.

Down the slope behind me was the pond with the tadpoles. All the tadpoles in our jar had to be dead by now, part of the landscape. Maybe birds had come by and scooped them up for food.

The train took a long time to pass. While I waited, and while the guy at my feet continued to moan and writhe, I considered what we were going to do next. I wanted everything to be right between us, between me and my friend, but I didn't know how to make that happen. My friend saved my life, but he also wanted this kid to die. I didn't blame him. Not really, but it was still a big difference between us. I wanted to hurt the kid. And I did do that. But I didn't want him to die. That was going too far. Not too far for my friend, though.

The train still squealed. The wheels still tried to stop. The cars were slowing down, but they weren't going to stop for a while. I guessed the engineer wanted to stop so he could see what happened.

I took several steps back from the train, down the slope of rocks and dirt and weeds. Then I turned and hurried my pace until I got to the pond. I ran around the rim of the pond and jumped over fallen logs and didn't stop. I kept going into the woods. The ground under my feet was soft. Layers of dead leaves, still moist from snow melt, carpeted the forest floor. Within a couple of minutes I was deep into a wooded land.

There was a lot I didn't want to face. I didn't want to see my friend again because I wasn't sure he was a friend. Not after he wanted some asshole kid to die. There's no doubt the kid was an asshole. But that didn't give us the right to kill him.

I kept returning to that thought. He deserved punishment, but how far to take that punishment? And were we the ones who should do it? It made sense. After all, we were friends and I got smacked in the head with a rock from the kid.

I also didn't want to face my parents and try to tell them what had happened. The whole story was crazy and they didn't understand what kids did anyway. Not really. And I also didn't want to deal with seeing a doctor. I would have to explain how stupid I was, looking up at some kid throwing rocks when I should have been keeping my head down. The woods seemed like the best place for me right then, and I thought why not try it for a while? Why not spend some time in a place that didn't want anything from me?

The train's fugue of clickety-clacks and wheel-squeals faded behind me, absorbed by the trees now surrounding me. Each step I took made my wound strain against my skin. It was like it was a creature of its own and it wanted to jump off me and run away. I put my hand up to it, to feel the contours of it. So fascinating to have a wound, especially one that insistently leaked blood. It was slick and warm. Rivulets of blood flowed away from it, like a river delta. My friend's sock had long since disappeared. I tried to remember what had happened to it but could not. The cut had taken something out of my brain, it seemed. Or was that even possible? No, it couldn't be.

The light had dimmed considerably. I kept walking. Trees around me felt close, as though they wanted to touch me as I walked by.

Our town had little presence of its own. It was a small piece of civilization plunked down in this wild land. The mine where my father worked was on the other side from where I was. The pond that my friend and I liked to visit was a wild thing itself. A nursery for frogs. On hot summer days last year, the frogs were so loud and insistent that I heard my parents grumbling about needing to go out and kill the green plague if they were going to get any sleep at all. A couple of enterprising families did go out and catch frogs and try to sell the legs, but didn't have much luck in town. They ended up eating them themselves.

I kept walking away from the pond. We had stories, the kids in school. Lots of tales that involved the woods where I was now. Some kids insisted there were more ponds, a whole string of them extending for miles into the forest. Other kids said the forest was littered with bears and they were all hungry. Kids were particularly attractive to their gastronomical instincts. And so on. Hardly anyone had actually gone far except some of the kids who went with their fathers in the fall, hunting for deer and sometimes elk. One kid shot a moose once.

I wasn't too worried about bears. Maybe I should have been. I had heard that if you make lots of noise, the bears stay away from you. As I walked I picked up twigs and broke them. The sound—a burst of snapping fibers—made me think of broken bones. The forest was littered with twigs, which maybe meant it was littered with the bones of dead things.

A crow wheeled overhead. I wiped dried blood from my face. It came off in powdery clumps.

The crows swooped down to my level and one strutted around in front of me. I stopped to watch it for a while. It cocked its beak in my direction and nodded at me, as though asking me for help. Or telling me a story. I wasn't sure which. Just as I was about to walk away from it, the crow rose up and spread its wings in front of me. I put up my hands, not in fear, because I was not afraid, but out of surprise. I wanted to protect my wound. I had an inkling that it was my weak spot now, the place that needed protection if I was to continue my life. The crow circled me a couple of times and eased down through the air and flapped its wings with stubborn energy, the wild life of it grabbing the aura around me and pulling it away from me for a moment. It was a defenseless instant for me. I let go whatever fortifications remained for me. My wound was open in more ways than one. The crow landed on the top of my head and bent down to the cut above my brow. It decided it wanted to investigate, I suppose. It ran its beak along the edges of the cut. I felt some pain, but not enough to matter. I had no notion of symbiosis at that time in my life, but I did understand that my moments with the crow were significant in some way I would not understand for a long time, if ever. Today, thinking back on that brief encounter, I feel only gratitude. Something in the way the crow seemed to understand my wound gave me sustenance at a time I needed support.

Its talons gripped my scalp, the points of them dug into me. I couldn't tell if they drew blood. I only knew they were like my friend's fingertips on the lid of the pollywog jar. My wound had crusted over some, but that didn't stop the crow from poking around in there. Maybe that made it poke around more. I don't know what it was looking for. Food, maybe? Did crows consume blood? Well, they ate everything, didn't they? Maybe this crow thought my crusty blood was a string of berries or something. At first I wanted to pull away from the thing, but then I didn't mind it poking away at my wound. In fact, it felt kind of good. I noticed some bugs had crawled up on there, like they were liking my blood, too. So maybe the crow was eating the bugs? I remembered something my teacher had said once, about symbioses. It was like different animals helped each other out just because it was good for both of them. So maybe that's what this crow was doing. I gave it blood that it liked, and it picked off bugs that I didn't want.

Every now and then the crow flapped its wings. That was a strange sound, like it was taking air and pulling it over its feathers. The feathers made this swishing noise. It was the kind of thing you didn't hear much and I was hearing it up close, as close as you could get.

The crow adjusted its feet so the talons ungripped my head and re-gripped it in a different position. That relief of pain and then the reinstating of pain felt peculiarly pleasant. I wondered if the crow was aware of the satisfaction its talons gave me.

The truth was that the crow was most likely completely uninterested in me as a person. I was just this thing in the woods that had a red gash that it was interested in. That was okay with me. One thing I noticed right away was that the pressure in my skull was much less intense than it had been. It was like the crow was relieving the force of my brain that had been trying to punch its way out of my head. I don't think I'm making that up from a distance of fifty years. I'm pretty sure that's exactly what I thought at the time. I had this notion that the rock had found a way into my head. Snaked its power right past my skull to my brain. Because at that age the world was more than mysterious. It was completely incomprehensible. Why were we all stuck out in these woods just so the fathers could pull up rocks from the ground? It didn't make sense. We should live in a real place and let the men drive to the mine. Didn't that make more sense? And why were we kids stuck in a stupid barn for hours at a time just so some teacher could tell us what she thought about the world? That didn't make any sense either. Wasn't it better to let us be out in the world? And church. We went to a church that Valton Mines had built for us. Almost everyone in town went. And what was that for? It was crazy for everyone to get together every Sunday when no one wanted to be there. Not really. You could see it. The way everyone had these expressions on their faces like they had eaten something rotten. The whole world didn't make any sense, and when nothing makes sense, then you need to make up things and that's what I did. I made up this story about the rock tunneling into my brain.

Maybe I was still a bit woozy. I'm not even to the most important part of the story.

See, this crow, it wasn't the only one. As I stood there with it picking at my wound, I chanced to look up and I saw a ring of crows, like a black-beaked Stonehenge, in a circle above me, each bird sitting in a tree and looking down at me. They were all completely still. The air around them was still. Everything felt like it was on hold. The forest. Time. My life. On hold until this one crow was finished doing whatever it was it needed to do with the blood encrusting my wound. My face had dried blood all over it. And my shirt looked like a warrior's uniform. I looked like someone who had been in the fight of his life. I wanted to take it off. Bare my chest to the forest. I had the urge, but something kept me from it, as though I didn't have the right to do so at that time. Or as though I knew my chest, thin and boyish, was not going to impress the forest on any level.

Eventually, the crow stopped its machinations and stretched its wings and extended its legs so its talons dug even deeper into my skull, making me wince, and then it flapped its wings, sent air cascading down my face and chest, and flew off. A chorus of wing rustles followed as all the crows decided to take to the air at once. The cloud of them rose higher above me. It was as though they were a column of smoke released from a chimney. They rose as one diffuse organism, and I envied the shape of that creature. I did not think about the individual crows, but rather the conglomeration of them, how they coalesced into a robust and singular entity all its own. I spun around as they spiraled up, and I put out my hands and tried to imitate their motions.

They headed in a direction away from Valton. I followed. My feet ran over spongy forest floor and then the land rose up and I was on rock. I burst above the tree line and stopped. The flock of crows kept going. I turned around and was startled to see the train, huffing and puffing like a paused dragon letting smoke loose upon the world, on the other side of the pond. It had come to a full stop and two men ran along the side of it and stopped and bent over a shape next to the train. That had to be the rock thrower. I looked for my friend, but I didn't see him anywhere. He must have run back home.

I saw the men's mouths moving, but could not hear a sound from them. They helped the kid sit up. I saw him clutching his side, like he was trying to keep his guts from falling out. I imagined how the conversation must be going. He was probably telling them that a couple of other kids attacked him for no reason and then ran away. I knew how these things worked. The guy who was really at fault rarely, if ever, got into trouble. The grown-ups never ever got the story straight and as often as not it was the guy who didn't do anything who got into trouble.

I kept low. I didn't want them to see me. Beyond the train, visible like a clump of twigs, the tangle seemed to beckon to me. I don't say this lightly, but with a certain understanding of its strange meaning. How could a pile of old trees beckon to anyone? Especially me. But as I recall it now, sitting at my desk composing this narrative, I vividly recall the way in which the crisscross pile seemed to be saying something to me. I didn't know what to think then, perhaps didn't even realize that the tangle had its eyes on me, but it didn't matter, because as soon as I felt the calling, I was determined to go to it.

I descended to the other side of the rocky hill, which put its mass between me and the train. I began walking north, through the snarl of downed branches and last year's dead ferns. Wildflowers would be coming up here later in the spring, but it was too early yet. The air was cold, as though someone had poured a vat of it down the rocky hill and it had all pooled at the bottom.

The sun was still high in the sky. I walked for ten or fifteen minutes, batting away branches and swatting at mosquitoes as I went.

The sky was an inverted blue bowl covering me and everything I knew. I felt as small as the tadpoles in the pond, almost aimlessly flitting about the pool of air that drowned Valton in its grip. My feet seemed to traverse the ground of their own accord, with me following along for the ride. I went over a rise, brushed along a stand of trees, waded through an ice-cold creek, and scared a few squirrels up the trunk of a pine tree, their tiny claws scratching at the bark like they were trying to relieve an itch. The crows had disappeared from my sight, but other birds, a woodpecker and tiny wrens, flitted about in the shadows surrounding me. My feet, wet and cold from the creek, squished under my legs. I walked over two more rises, my fevered need to keep going was something I could not abate.

I stopped on the top of a rock prominence, and panted for air. In the distance I saw the corrugated sheet metal of the structures housing the mine shafts. They looked like misplaced toy blocks in this wooded setting. Beyond the mine shafts, a long tall building, dirty with caked soil and dust, squatted against the green woods. Next to that, a large parking lot, filled with the cars of the miners who drove the four miles from town. So strange for them to go such a short distance. They hardly needed cars, I often thought. Why not just have the miners bused from town to the mine?

I asked my father that once and he looked at me like I was something he needed to scrape off the bottom of his shoe. I don't get in a bus, he said.

But why not, Dad? I asked.

The bus is for poor people. You think we're poor people?

I didn't know if we were or if we weren't. I knew that we weren't happy people. Not by a long way. I don't think I knew what being happy would feel like.

But it wouldn't be like a real bus, I said. The company would provide it for you. It would just be for workers.

Where we come from, said my father, if you get on a bus you are the lowest of the low. You understand?

I didn't. My parents often talked about the old country. How it was so different. I didn't know anything about it. I was born in Valton, a year or so after my parents moved here. My father brought my mother there for the job. Physical labor was about the best thing someone from the old country could hope for if they didn't know the language and had no other real skills. Not that my father wasn't a capable person, but he was from a different society with different ways. I think I vaguely understood all that at the time, but only in a piecemeal way. It was the same way I understood the great world outside the perimeter of Valton: I knew it existed, but its parameters were difficult to pin down.

If you didn't have the car, I said, we could use that money for other things.

Things that you want, huh? he said.

Not just me. You and Mom.

Uh huh, he said. And what is it that you want?

What I really wanted was a bicycle, but I knew better than to ask for that. I was thinking, I said, it would be nice to have a telescope.

Again, the look, like he didn't know what species I might be a part of. A telescope? What you want a telescope for?

To look at the stars and the planets. It gets so dark here,

Dad. There's no city lights. In cities you can't look at the stars because it isn't dark enough.

Okay okay, he said. Such weariness in his voice that even I, at age nine, could tell. Maybe a telescope, he said. Maybe.

I liked hearing that. I imagined having the thing. I wanted to look through it and discover comets and asteroids. I didn't know why I wanted to do that, but the thought of even getting close filled me with a joy that I don't believe I have experienced since then. I have had other joys, but nothing like that anticipation. It had a kind of pure innocence about it, like the only thing that mattered was the sky. Before the awakening to the possibilities and murkiness of human interaction, I had that inkling of clarity.

But the telescope never came. I believe I knew it would never come, even when my father said it would come. It was a lie we both accepted but did not acknowledge.

As I descended back down the hill I began to regret the absence of a telescope in my life. I saw it as a deeply unfair development that no such object had made it into my possession. My friend, the one who would not help me save the rock thrower's life, when I told him about how much I wanted a telescope said with a matter-of-fact deadpan voice, that I would outgrow a telescope in no time, so why even bother with getting one. Eventually I would want a car and girls. I should bide my desires until such time as those yearnings came to fruition. Then all my energy could be directed toward satisfying those wants.

My friend baffled me regularly. When he spoke in such a way about my future was one of those times and I told him that he didn't know what he was talking about. And then he told me that I needed to look around at the world because that's the way it was. Everyone wanted a mate and everyone wanted a car. It was a fact. I wondered if he had gotten a hold of the book but I didn't dare ask him because I was afraid he would think I was hopelessly ignorant to think there even was such a book.

I suppose a lot of us have that kind of friend in our childhoods, the person who always seems to know more than you do, who always conveys an air of deep wisdom, even when you know they can't possibly have that kind of wisdom. Not at age nine, anyway.

Such strange thoughts for a kid. We're told children should be children, which seems to mean they shouldn't have any troubles or responsibilities. But all conscious beings have troubles. It's impossible to avoid.

Still. Was I really such a melancholy and introspective boy, or am I projecting my current personality onto my nascent character at the time? So hard to tell from this distance. I feel as though I'm looking through a kind of telescope back at myself, one built from a tube of time with memories for lenses. And everyone knows memories are imperfect, shot through with distortions and blemishes that alter what you see. Or think you see.

It had gotten much warmer. I had traveled a long way on foot. The woods had passed by me as I thought of my life and my friend. I was missing my friend, even though we had been separated for only a short time. And even though I had serious quibbles with how he handled the situation with the rock thrower. We usually did this sort of thing together, out in the woods, tromping around aimlessly. It was a way to spend the time. Now I was spending this time on my own and I wasn't sure how to proceed. It was as though I was a stranger here with my head wound and my solitary presence. I waded across another stream and came to a hill of gravel, which I soon realized had been put there by some kind of heavy machinery. I climbed up the hill, knocking rocks aside so they rolled down and sent up dust that invaded my lungs and caused irritation in my cut. I wanted to scratch the gash, but refrained, intuiting, I suppose, that it would not have been a healthy course of action for me.

At the top of the gravel I came to a level area with the two corrugated mine shaft enclosures in the distance. I remember thinking how surprising it was that I had come up to them so quickly, since they had seemed a long way off only a few minutes before. Conveyer belts rose up on spindly legs from the shafts to the top of a building further away, which I knew was the mill where the ore got crushed before being loaded into box cars and hauled away by train. I walked toward the mill, passing the parking lot where all the dads parked their cars when they reported to work for the mine. I looked for my father's car but couldn't find it among all the rest. The cars reminded me of marshmallows, the way they sat all puffy and soft-looking, like

I could reach out and poke a hole in them. The mill displayed a gaping black doorway, big enough for tall and wide trucks to drive in. I went to that door and stood quietly, aware of my small size next to the cavernous dark entrance way. I heard noises of machinery coming from inside. A rush of cool wind exiting the mill and I had this inkling of the interior creating its own weather system, like it was another world. The air over my wound felt like a soothing ointment, the way it calmed the pain into something different from pain. Like a patch that had been sewn on my forehead. It took me a long time to make up my mind, but eventually I got up the courage to walk into the mill, which seemed like such a forbidden place that my heart beat almost uncontrollably. I thought I was violating something so basic that I would not have been surprised if guillotine blades fell upon me as I stepped over the threshold.

Here was my father's realm. The place that took him from the family everyday. What was the attraction?

The interior was cool, like stepping into a fridge. My eyes took a few minutes to adjust to the darkness. I stood, waiting for the world of the mill to move itself out of the dark gloom and into my consciousness. My whole being was alive with excitement. I felt it in my fingers and my knees, the way the joints seemed to take on the weight of the world. I had never been here before. My father said when I got older I might want to work in the mine, but I never thought I would see the mill before then.

The walls rose up at least three stories. To my eyes it seemed like nothing could be bigger. If anything ever dared try to attain a larger size, it would have to collapse under its own hubris. The clamor of conveyer belts rattling with muck and rubble swirled around me. They crisscrossed the space above and before me, like they were slicing the air into more manageable segments. I tried to follow the routes of the belts, but their destinations were lost in the darkness that this space seemed to collect into great patches here and there.

Great towers bulked up out of the floor and rose to the roof, dizzyingly high above my head. I saw shadowy things flying way up there, darting in and out of my vision. I thought they were birds. That they must have gotten trapped here. Or did they want to be here, like me?

A man with a yellow hard hat and a shovel over his shoulder stood on a metal grating some distance up and away from me. He studied me carefully and I waved at him. He nodded slightly and waved back. Something in the air changed with those two waves. I wasn't on an adventure anymore. I had been seen and I couldn't make the man unsee me.

He cupped his hands to his mouth and must have shouted something to me, but I couldn't hear him, and pretended I didn't see he was trying to talk to me. I looked away and began walking along the wall. He leaned over the railing and shouted at me some more but I hurried my pace and tried to get out of his view. Then I heard his boots clonk on the grating as he ran to intercept me. I ducked into the interior of the mill and began running as fast as I could, dodging the struts and beams that supported the network of conveyer belts looping the air above me.

Now I began to feel the sound of the place as a personal thing. The noise was beyond anything I had ever encountered before. It not only displaced all other sounds, including my own breath and voice, it seemed to choke out the energy in the room as well. It was like I was riding on a wave of sound in a sea of unimaginable power. The vibrations shook my bones and lodged in my chest. I imagined that I could ride on that wave. But just as I was getting ready to jump and catch hold of the passing surge, it all stopped.

All of it.

The conveyer belts halted. The rocks stopped rattling, the gears that drove the belts simply stopped turning. All that motion and energy, abruptly halted, made me stop too. I stood frozen on the floor, one foot poised to step forward, and held that pose for I don't know how long. It seemed like ages and ages, but it couldn't have been. That must be my own projection onto my past. Just as I was thinking about putting my foot on the floor, two powerful arms wrapped themselves around me from behind. My own arms got clamped to my sides and a rage erupted in me like I had never known before. I screamed and tried to push the clamping force away from me, but I could not budge it. I felt panic invade me and dizziness seize my reason. I kept pushing, straining every muscle in my body, but it was no use at all. I could not move the arms holding me. Everything seemed too precarious, like I was going to die. That's what it felt like. I was sure that my death was going to happen right here in the mill where my father worked.

Now don't be that way, kid. A voice from behind me.

Let me go, I said.

Nothing doing. I'm going to hang onto you until the shift boss comes. They'll be here soon, since I shut down the belts. They'll want to know what's up.

Obviously, there was no way a nine-year-old was going to fight a powerful man determined to keep him in check, but that didn't stop me from trying. I hardly felt like myself, the way some unaccountable will seemed to be doing the pushing for me. That will pushed with all the power of the universe, so it seemed to me. My legs kicked backwards. The man lifted me up and I kicked only air, which frustrated me and made me even more determined to fight him. My face must have been red. He laughed, which made me even more angry.

I have a cut, I screamed at the walls and ceilings.

That stopped him.

Cut? he said.

Yeah. Put me down.

I'll put you down, kid, but you have to promise you won't run off.

My breaths puffed air like a train vibrating on tracks, huffing the world into its engines. I promise, I said.

He seemed doubtful. Why shouldn't he be? But he let me down on the concrete floor of the mill. My feet touched the hard surface and I had every intention of bolting from him as soon as he released me. Instead, he kept a hold of my shoulders and I had no choice but to wait there, at least for a few minutes. I had my head tilted down so he couldn't see my face.

Show me where you're cut, he said.

I turned to him and lifted my chin so my forehead was displayed for him.

He whistled. Where'd you get that? he said.

In a fight.

He got that satisfied look I knew he would get. Not bad, he said. How'd the other guy end up?

Way worse than this, I said. He's really fucked up. Miner's language seemed the only appropriate mode of communication right then.

The guy laughed. You shouldn't use that word kid.

Fuck, I said. Fuck fuck fuck.

He laughed again and put out a hand and moved it like he was patting down a mound of earth, shaping it into a smooth pile. Okay okay, he said. I get it. You're revved up from your fight. You live in Valton?

Yeah, I said. Where else would I live?

Don't know. Whose kid are you, anyway?

I told him my father's name. He got a flash of recognition in his eyes. Oh yeah, he said. I know him. He works underground. What the hell are you doing here?

Let me go and I'll tell you.

He still had me gripped by the shoulders. I felt him loosen his hold very slightly. If I do, you have to promise you won't run off.

Promise, I said.

He dropped one arm and put his hand around my wrist and held it tightly. He dropped his other arm and I leaned forward and spit in his face and kicked him in the ankles as hard as I could. He let me go more from surprise than from me overpowering him in any way. He threw out some miner's language of his own and I bolted from him and began running back the way I had come, toward the big door with its now blinding slab of light beckoning me to the outside.

Once out of the mill, I angled my path north, back to the woods. I heard shouts behind me and turned my head without slowing my pace. I saw three or four men coming after me, but they would never catch me. They were all three of them weighed down with heavy boots, hard hats, and thick clothes. They tried to run, but they weren't doing a very good job of it.

Come back here, kid, I heard one of them say.

You want get into some trouble?

The funny thing was, I did want to get into some trouble and I didn't know why. I passed the tailing pools, two big reservoirs that held the leftover tailings from the milling operation. They looked like gloppy other world things, gray and bubbling in parts, and an almost phosphorescent white in others. These pools of tailings, the by-product of most mining operations, were filled with toxic materials and mining companies just poured them into the land. Tailing pools like them were the source of much consternation years later when people woke up to the fact that they just might possibly be an environmental and health hazard.

I knew none of that then. I only knew the pools obviously had something to do with the mining of uranium and thought they were amazing looking. I wanted to stop and study them. Maybe wade into them, or float homemade boats on them. I might even have had a notion to swim in them. The odor wafting from them was mud and metal and something I couldn't identify, like what might have permeated a battlefield. I knew nothing of battlefields, obviously, but that was the thought that came to my young mind. I thought also that my father was partly responsible for this mess. It was like I wanted to experience what my father experienced and I didn't know why. My mother said my father sacrificed himself for his family. He worked this terrible job doing this dangerous thing—experiencing dangers she didn't even understand but knew were there—just so we could eat and have shelter.

My parents did not always get along, and our life was miserable in many ways, but even so, I was expected to be grateful to my father for choosing this way of life for us.

I didn't understand, obviously, how these things worked, how adults made choices that resonated all through their lives and their children's lives. I also didn't care, for the most part, but seeing those tailing pools somehow made the choices real. We weren't forced to live where we lived, not really. We picked Valton.

I think I wanted to immerse myself in the essence of Valton, and there was some mystical thing inside me that suggested this was that essence, spread out in a toxic mess.

I observed it for perhaps five seconds. What happened in those five seconds I can't properly say, now, but something changed in my world. Recall the pond where me and my friend had collected tadpoles. That was a pool of unsurprising grace and beauty, even though I barely knew those terms at the time. But these tailing pools were nothing like the pond at all, even though I had heard my father call them ponds. I observed the gray dead expanse of them and thought of my brain, the mushy mess of that thing. I had seen a picture of the brain in class once. It didn't seem that the picture I saw had anything to do with what was supposed to be the amazing power of the human mind. And so it was with these tailing ponds. They didn't seem to have anything to do with the natural world, though the material that filled them had come from the earth, about as natural a world as anyone could find anywhere.

I wanted to imagine creatures, like mutant tadpoles, maybe, swimming around in that sludge, but try as I might, I could not conjure up the image of them. I looked across the pool to the far shore, propped up against the woods with a concrete rim. A raccoon scampered across the top of the rim. I watched it with fascination, wondering if it was going to dive into the pool, or if it was looking for some other place to be. I opened my being to everything around me at that moment. Though I understand that my recounting these events so long after the fact may be distorting my memories and perceptions of them.

Behind me, I heard big clunky men still clomping the ground in my pursuit. I began running again and shot between the two pools and came out on the other side where the tracks expanded into three parallel pairs of tracks. Box cars waited in patient rows to be filled up with the uranium ore. There were dozens of the cars, lined up like toys. I saw a mill worker walking along them. He carried a long metal tool with which he could move the cars himself, one lone man rolling tons of metal along a track. So many people doing their part in the operation. I had no idea until then what it took to keep the mine process going.

The man looked up at me as I passed by. More of the world flowered in my brain. His look was surprise and indignation all at the same time. Who was that? And what was he doing here? He called to me but I ignored him. I angled my feet away from him just as he realized I was being pursued by his co-workers and that perhaps he should be chasing me as well.

He never did. I increased my speed. My hands pumped hard and my legs carried me with a gratifying pace into the protection of the trees in the forest. I jumped over fallen logs, bent my head sideways to avoid overhanging limbs and skirted roots that bulged out of the ground like limbs reaching for the sky. Nothing, it seemed, was going to stop me.

Which was a strange turn of events, considering that up until then I was the kind of kid who rarely did anything that would cause my elders much trouble at all. I felt the strange freedom of defiance permeate my being but its alien weight in my muscles could not stop my motion through the trees.

What I remember most from those minutes was not the men pursuing me—after all, they could not catch me—but the presence of this alien inside me. In the normal course of events, my friend and I would have taken our tadpoles and spent the rest of the afternoon observing them, or ignoring them. But when the rock hit me, my world changed. It was not just the injury and the blood, but also the unleashing of my fury upon the boy who threw the rock. I wanted to hurt him. If he had died from my kicks I would not have cared. I'm sure, in fact, that I would have been very happy.

This was a completely different mode of being for me. I was the kid who never got into fights, who never argued with anyone, who never wanted to engage physically with bullies, and so on. I was the kid who always looked for the easier road, the one that did not run into anyone else.

So now, adrift on an unfamiliar sea with an unfamiliar attitude and way of being, it was almost acceptable to be inundated with the strange sensation of another being inside me. This double, which seemed to fit snugly and well inside my person, had the relentless drive that I did not. He snaked his way into my limbs and permeated my muscles. He entwined his being around my being. Not my soul. That aspect of me, whatever it was, seemed to remain impervious to his influence, but my physical, mechanical self, the part of me made of hinged and socketed bones, supported by clumps of protein, that was completely open to him.

I also felt as though he had been there for some time, and I had only just noticed him, the way one notices a picture on the wall, suddenly, after years of living with it. It pops out of the background and makes you see it, suddenly.

In any case, whatever it or he was, or whatever it thought itself to be, it ran me over the fern- and leaf-strewn floor of the forest. He took me away from the mill with haste and grace. I flew between the trunks of the trees. I thought that if I merely exerted my will, my double would lift me up and over the trees, soaring on the wind like a dandelion seed.

I heard distant and subdued grunts and puffing breaths behind me. Even a few snapped branches as the pursuing miners tried to get closer to me. I felt wonder at my youth. How it gave me the advantage in this race. Not to mention my robust need to preserve myself from their inevitable grown-up questions and accusations. This was what I mostly did not want to endure. I would get enough shame from my parents when all this came to an end, but in the meantime I didn't need to have even more humiliation heaped upon me. Better to keep it confined to our company-built household.

I did look ahead to the conclusion of my odyssey, trying to discern an end game in all this, but no details came to mind at that time. I saw the future as an endlessly receding event, moving away from me with relentless speed, so that the inevitable moment when I was to be captured or stopped, in my mind, would never come. Probably my first inkling of an infinite series. I rediscovered the ancient paradox of the Greeks, which stated that one could never finish a race, because to get to a point a mile away, one had to get to a point half a mile away. And to get to that point, one had to get to a point one quarter miles away. To get to that point, a runner had to get to a point one-eighth of a mile away. And so on for infinity. There were an infinity of points to get to, and therefore it would take an infinite amount of time to traverse all of them. Therefore, it was impossible to cover any length in a finite amount of time.

A future professor of mathematics encountered the reality and unreality of an infinite series as a child. I didn't even know then that what I was doing was mathematics. My conception of math at that time did not extend much beyond arithmetic. But I felt a thrill in my bones thinking about the strangeness of not being able to cover a distance, yet, by empirical evidence, contradicting that, because, obviously, people ran distances all the time.

My double seemed to laugh at me. That is, I thought I heard him laugh, a voice in my head that was not my own. You want to work out puzzles or you want to run? it said. It's up to you, but if I was you, I'd run. Run for all you're worth.

He was like a suit of clothes that I put on. He didn't feel like me at all, but rather felt like something I wore. Something that sunk its limbs into mine. A suit of clothes that had other features, things that no article of clothing ever had. And yet, it all seemed as natural as water. It was the way I was made.

I asked my double if we could stop for a bit.

Why would you want to stop? he asked. Why would anyone want to stop running?

I need to stop, I said. I'm getting tired. I want to see where we are.

We went on for a few more steps, then he slowed his pace abruptly. I lurched to a standing position, almost falling over in the process as my knees went weak and my arms wanted to emulate rubber bands.

I stood panting for breath.

I think they stopped chasing me, I said to my double.

My double didn't answer at first. Then: I think you're right. What did you do that they wanted to catch you?

I turned around to survey my surroundings. I was in a small clearing, a meadow. I learned in school that meadows were former lakes that had been filled in over time. I liked the idea of standing in a lake that wasn't there anymore. The usual trees circled the meadow. I wondered how many trees this landscape surrounding Valton needed. There seemed to be an endless expanse of them. I turned around. Just over the tops of the trees, I saw the very top of the Valton shafts, corrugated sheet metal caps like small hats on the trees.

I kicked a guy, I said out loud in a barely audible whisper.

Tsk tsk, said my double. You some kind of bad kid?

I felt my face flush. Was I a bad kid? I didn't think so. No, I said. I don't do things like that.

Well I didn't do it.

I know, I said. The guy tried to kill me. It made me crazy.

Tried to kill you, huh? said the voice. That's hard to believe. He some kind of crazy kid?

Must be, I said.

How about you, then? my double asked. Maybe you're not a bad kid, but maybe you're some kind of crazy kid?

No! Why do you keep asking me?

I'm trying to figure out why you created me. Why did I all of a sudden begin orchestrating your movements? You know, most people, if they knew what was happening, would say that you were losing your mind. You think you're losing your mind?

None of this conversation was something a nine-year-old should be dealing with. At least, I don't think so. I don't think anyone should have to be conducting arguments with mysterious voices.

As I recount the events in this narrative, removed by years

from their origin, I think of some of my students in my classes over the years. There were a few who displayed a certain double life, an attitude that had them physically present, while mentally elsewhere. It's a common observation of teachers everywhere, as I am aware, but it always troubled me to see it. I thought that such a splitting of one's personality had to be detrimental to the person being split. Nothing in my years of teaching persuaded me otherwise. I am convinced that we were all meant to be one coherent entity, doing one thing at a time with one mind and body. None of us are multitaskers, though some of us believe we can be. As I progressed through my teaching years, indeed, as I progressed through my life, I heard many people—friends, colleagues, students, strangers—say that they wished they had one thing they could be proud of in their lives. Or they said that there was only one thing they wanted to be in their lives. And so on. I don't think this attitude is an accident. One is the minimum. Not zero. Zero is nothing. One is everything.

Forgive my mystical bent, it's the crutch of an old man. As the end draws near, the compulsion to see beyond the finish line makes people my age a little loopy. It makes it doubly perilous to be bringing a kid's life and attitude to the fore in this narrative. I'm struggling with finding the truth of that time, and keeping the truth of this time away from it. To keep its purity as much possible.

God created the integers, as the saying goes. Everything else is the doing of mathematicians.

I always liked that saying. Gave me a feeling of power that was probably unwarranted. We math folks just push around symbols on paper, after all.

When I was conversing with my double, all those years ago, it seemed both strange and not strange, which I took to be a warning that the whole enterprise was not sustainable. How to maintain those contradictory stances simultaneously? I wanted the double to be gone. I asked him to leave.

His answer, or, more properly, response, was to laugh. I felt the laugh in my joints and my muscles. It coursed through me like a spark of relentless flame, sustained by the fuel of my incredulity. It made my head light. It put pressure on my wound.

I didn't like that laugh. Didn't like that it was supported by my own being as much as by the independent will of my double.

Then, awkwardly but decisively, my double determined that we should be moving in a new direction. It spun me around with decisive power. It was as though it had turned a windup gear to build tension and then abruptly released it. I barely kept up with my footwork—I danced on tiptoes to remain upright in my pirouette—and stumbled away from Valton again, going deeper into the forest, in an easterly direction, away from the mill and the town and towards who knew what.

Ahead of me was only wilderness for miles. I had little conception of the vastness of Northern Ontario, only knew that if I went far enough, I would get to polar bears and Eskimos. The Arctic Ocean. Persistent snow and ice. Not that I thought

I would encounter any of those things on that day, but the thought still intrigued me.

I noted the closing gap between the sun and the horizon. It would soon be dark, and a chill was already in the air. But nothing I did could stop my feet from churning forward, my arms from swinging with decisive motion, and my body from leaning forward into the future.

I continued like this for some time. How long is difficult to say. I entered some kind of trance state, tempered by fatigue and tired muscles, as well as thirst and hunger. My path took me deep into the woods. I entered thick groupings of trees. The light from the sun became a kind of solid substance, hanging like yellow foam above me, snagged on the tips of trunks and combed by rough bark.

Years later I would enter a cathedral and the vaulted ceilings, with light streaming in through the stained glass windows set almost to ceiling height, would remind me of that moment in the woods. My double stopped us and made me look around. Was I in awe? Who can say now. I still hold the image of that light, though, still feel it like an enveloping womb, all soft and warm, but giving. Tangles of spider web drifted through the air, illuminated into strings of dazzling light. Dust motes, some as big as bees, floated like constellations over me. The deep silence of my surroundings was broken only by my own breathing, taking in that solid light and air, and releasing it with a rapidity and force that made me think of when I kicked the rock thrower.

Don't think about that, said my double.

How do you know what I'm thinking?

Never mind that. I know that you want to go to the cemetery where your sister is.

My sister's dead, I said, as though I was telling him something shocking, something that would snap him out of his authoritative stance.

Of course she is, dummy, he said. She's dead. It's a cemetery. Funny how those two things go together, isn't it?

I don't want to go there, I said.

He ignored me and moved me through the cathedral to the other side. The light had already begun to fade. We rose up on a long sloped escarpment that allowed an angled climb. The rock felt good under my feet, like I had something to hold onto that was solid, more solid than the thing directing my motion. But I noticed that even my double was a little tired.

When does your father get off his shift? he asked.

I had to think. This was his night shift week, when he came home after I went to bed. Midnight, I said.

It's going to be sooner than that, he said.

What are you talking about? I said.

We're missing, now. Runaways. They're going to tell your mother and she's going to want your father with her. To help look for us and because she's scared when he goes underground and she's going to be even more scared with you missing.

I'm only missing because you made me run away, I said.

Not true, he said. You began the run, I only continued it.

I didn't know about semantics back then, but I recognized this as an argument with no substance, just a difference in our perception of the events that occurred.

You could take me back to the miners, I said. You could do it right now. I was starting to see that I didn't want to be out here much longer, not with night coming on. I was already cold and it was only going to get colder.

He seemed to consider the possibility of going back to the miners, then rejected it. I don't think so, he said.

I thought about my mother. I knew she got scared. All the wives in town were afraid for their husbands being in the ground under all those tons of rock. She talked about it, how they were all scared all the time. How they tried to keep busy so they wouldn't think about it. She knew stories about miners dying in cave-ins. She kept those stories to herself, mostly. She certainly never told me, but I heard about them.

My shadow was probably right that she would try to get my father to come back up, but I also knew that didn't always work. It wasn't easy to bring miners up at unscheduled times and the bosses tried to avoid it as much as they could. But my mother could probably make them. When she was determined, she usually got her way. My father would be pretty angry if he had to come up just because I was being a pain. They'd dock him his pay for the time he wasn't working.

They're still upset about my sister, I said to my double.

So?

It's not nice to be giving them something else to worry about.

He laughed. You worry about them?

Sometimes.

They should be worried about you. That's the way it works.

I just don't think we need to upset them anymore, I said.

Being upset is part of being a parent. It's what they signed up for when they had you. We can use that. Especially if we don't turn into a cry baby.

I didn't like that he was referring to me as we when there was no we, not in any way that counted.

The horizon, studded as it was with tall trees, did not offer me any kind of relief from my torment, and torment it was, at least to me at the time. I looked to it the way I now look to the future, for some sense of the grand vision of the universe, some indication that there is more to the world than me. Not that I ever find consolation or relief from the curse of living. There are only small moments of peace in a chaotic sea of living. That's what years of mathematical training and life as a mathematics instructor has done for me: merely validated my early impulses that the future was a sad place.

Or so I now believe. The hardest part of recounting these events is sorting out what I know now with what I knew then. Surely this is the issue with all memoir? It seems reasonable, but

I don't know for sure, since this is the first memoir I've ever attempted.

But I did have anguish, even so young. I felt the futility of believing in expansive horizons when I was confined to the tiny life of Valton.

My double, who I began to think of as my shadow, did not help my anguish, though I think I turned to him for precisely that kind of help. I had not seen my sister but I had seen her grave. Surely the knowledge of her short existence was enough for me? Did I have to be made to see the finality of her demise?

Now here I was on the cusp of a monumental change in my life, though I did not recognize it at the time. I only thought that I was deluded, or perhaps had gone bonkers. Something. I will try to render the events as accurately as possible.

I turned my gaze away from the horizon, away, as it were from my future, or from some possible future. The air around me was electric with an energy I did not recognize. It had some of the quality of the atmosphere surrounding me when I kicked the rock thrower, but it was more intense, like it wanted to wrap itself around me and squeeze something out of me. What that might be, I could not say, but the very substance of existence seemed more alive with possibility than was healthy for anyone, especially me.

Why are you interested in me? I asked my shadow.

Because of us, he said. Because you are me.

Because I am you? I said.

Yes, I answered. Because I am you.

You are not me, he said.

Oh yes, I said. Yes I am.

There it is. The transition. It happened in that moment. Did you catch it? My skin has raised bumps all over me as I write the words.

It was so subtle at the time that I barely noticed and it was happening to me. I was no longer the nine-year-old who had been bonked on the head with a spinning rock. No, I was now the entity who was controlling that nine-year-old.

I told the kid that I was him, but that wasn't exactly right. It was simply the most easily told lie. And there's nothing wrong with lies, no matter what people try to tell you. No matter what they especially try to tell nine-year-olds, while still lying to them. All the time. I saw that right away, as soon as I transitioned to the shadow.

Hey kid, I said, you getting tired of this?

The kid nodded. He was breathing heavily. He had all those biological machinations going on, keeping his apparatus running. It was annoying, let me tell you. And not annoying in an interesting way. Annoying in the kind of way that kills all the life in a person. I took that to be my fault, I suppose. I kind of killed the life in him, didn't I, by becoming his shadow? By moving his presence out of his accustomed body and into the shadow self that was me.

The thing is, I couldn't quite get rid of him. Not completely.

I felt myself stretch and push out of him. Felt my presence lifting out of him the way a moth lifts out of a cocoon, but I couldn't quite pull all of myself all the way out. It was as though the cocoon had teeth and they were clamped to my big toe and they wouldn't let go, not for the briefest instant.

For myself, now that I was the shadow, there seemed absolutely no reason to remain tethered to the boy. What could he have to interest me? Was I not now a free spirit? I thought so. I had the feeling that I was. The world had grown by several orders of magnitude within a few seconds. I thought I could probably go to the moon if I had a mind to do so.

But he wouldn't let me go.

And here I had to ask myself why. When I was in the kid's position, I would have wanted nothing more than to let the shadow go. Yet here he was, holding on for dear life, as though there was nothing more important.

You know I'm not you anymore, don't you kid?

Stop calling me kid, he said. Of course I know what's going on here. I'm growing up and part of me is breaking off. Isn't that the way it happens?

Kid had no idea. None. He thought chunks of people broke off as they got older? Man. Sheltered life and all that. Only explanation for such a cockeyed conception of life.

He was trying to be brave. It was charming, in its way, but it was so inadequate. Like a fish bumping against the glass of an aquarium. Nothing more futile.

They're going to be giving you a hard time, I said to the kid.

He seemed resigned to that. I know, he said. I'm in big trouble.

No reason for me to be in trouble with you, I said.

He seemed puzzled. But they won't know about you, he said.

They could, I said.

So what do you want? he said.

Let me go.

I'm not stopping you.

You are stopping me. You're not releasing me to my freedom.

He straightened up. I let him think he had some kind of autonomy of his own. Not because I cared about him. But because I thought he might be more prone to giving me what I wanted if he thought he had some power of his own.

I'm not doing it on purpose, he said.

I couldn't argue with that. He didn't know enough about what was going on to actually make decisions counter to either of us. Also, to be as honest as possible, I wasn't exactly sure what was going on, either. We were still connected, that was clear. But the nature of the connection, the full import of our bond, that was still something of a mystery.

But mysteries are where knowledge starts. And knowledge is the source of everything, isn't it? Without knowledge there's no life, not really. Just existence. That's what I used to tell my students, in my more loopy days. They'd look mystified, wondering why I abandoned a perfectly comprehensible proof to take a side trip along some addled philosophical meanderings. I think I was an absent-minded professor long before I attained the age that justified such a stance. But it is true, as I insisted to my students. Knowledge brings all your experience together. Brings it to a place where you can pick it up and examine it. Even mathematical proofs are just distilled knowledge. From the book. I talked about the book. Not the book I thought existed when I was a kid. The other book. The one with all the best proofs for all the theorems that ever existed. The book written by the cosmic mathematicians. All math people were looking for the proofs from that book. You might call it our divine purpose, pulling out of that book the most concise and beautiful.

Oh, I'm rambling again. A consequence of my age and this narrative, how it tumbles the words and memories out of me. Let me just say that at the critical junction I'm talking about now, I thought I had much more autonomy than I ultimately did. I thought I could leap out of the kid and—I don't know— flit about the world, fly to mountaintops, dive into the ground and muck about there for a time. I had these fantasies. Born of the strange genesis of my spirit, I suppose, but ultimately, fantasies they were. I never left the kid. Ever. We were tied together. Even as he grew, I was still there. The kid is still with me, even as I write this. He knows I'm here. Sometimes he likes having me close by. Other times, he pretends he doesn't remember me and we have our separate lives, like married couples who don't talk. Other times I think he actually does forget about me and that's okay with both of us. After all, it can be draining to always have to acknowledge the existence of a strange spirit in your life.

But at the time. In my first few minutes and hours of life, the call of the great wide expanse of existence was overpowering. I wanted to fly. I wanted to leave the cocoon behind.

It's getting dark, he said.

Not my fault, I said.

I need to get home.

I sensed fear in his voice. And why shouldn't he be scared? He had no shelter and had never spent a night in the woods before. Much less alone in the woods.

Take me home, he said. I know you can do it. Take me.

Let me go, I said, and you can go home on your own.

I don't know how, he said.

More fear. With a tinge of whininess, which did not do his cause any good. I wasn't more inclined to help him based on his whimpering.

And here I did a cruel thing. Perhaps the worst thing I had done to anyone. I elected not to help him out of his predicament. I reasoned that if he was scared enough, something in him would figure a way to release me.

Nope, I said. Nothing doing. I'm not taking you back. You're getting out on your own, or you're staying here tonight. No other options.

He rebelled against that. He pushed against me. I felt his muscles and bones straining against my will. No way that his mass was going to budge my spirit. Spirit was always going to win, but I had to admire his tries. They were desperate, sure, but also concentrated. He had strength. A determination. Only thing is, so did I. I didn't want him attached to me.

After several minutes of trying to push me into a course of action I was determined not to take, he relaxed, exhaled long hard breaths, and told me I was a fucking shit and that he would never do something like this to anyone else.

I know, I said. I'm your opposite.

He muttered something about the book. I remembered the book. He thought what was happening to him was from the book. So strange, to hear what were once my thoughts coming back to me in this way. Was I really so ridiculous only a few short moments ago? Yes, it appears I was.

If you're so smart, he said, why can't you figure a way to split us up.

When did I say I was smart.

You don't have to say it, he said. I can tell you think it.

He had a point.

I don't know what's going on, I said. One of the mysteries of life, I suppose. You probably don't really want me gone, because then you'd be alone. So we're stuck with each other. Time to stop complaining about your predicament—our predicament—and take steps to ensure your survival.

He sighed and looked around. The world was shadow grey. It was already too late to collect wood and make a fire. Certainly much too late to catch any animal for his nourishment. The best he could do now was to hunker down somewhere reasonably dry and sheltered and hope he didn't get too cold in the night. I told him as much.

Then what should happen, but he started crying. That interrupted all my plans. He wasn't supposed to cry. What was he? Three years old?

Stop it, kid, I said.

He blubbered and sobbed. Made spastic hiccuping noises, like he was about to shake himself apart, like a machine with a screw loose, threatening to spread metal parts everywhere.

Stop it, kid, I said again, this time more sharply. You aren't helping yourself.

Then the flood gates opened. He stopped pretending to keep it all inside himself and he let loose with uninhibited bawling. He opened his mouth and wailed at the sky. I want my mommy, he said.

His mommy.

Well.

What was I supposed to do with that? I wanted him to keep crying. Figured it might give him the emotional energy and pull he needed to break the link between us. But here's the awful thing. His pain didn't remain inside him. It leaked out. Squirmed out, more like it. It was this rubbery thing, pliant and tough, grabbing up the world as it emerged from his body. The pain wrapped me up in itself and began sinking its weird appendages into me, like I was just a cushion for its pins. Before long, I started wailing for my mother. His mother. Our mother, I guess. The mother we both had and both missed.

We must have been quite a sight and sound out there in the dark Northern Ontario woods. Probably too ridiculous for the wild creatures to bother with.

After a while we both stopped our wails. We blubbered on with our sobs for a while longer. He wiped the snot off his nose with his sleeve, and seemed to think that our little mutual pity fest was going to give him some kind of reprieve.

Uh-uh. Didn't happen. I still had a goal. I wanted out.

You going to take me back now? he said.

I didn't answer right away. Instead, I gathered my energy and will around me, tightly, because I knew I was going to need it. I told him with as even and straight an expression as I could, that no, I was not going to take him back. He had to learn to fend for himself.

And here a remarkable thing happened. He accepted his situation. Not with snarkiness or any kind of attitude, either. He accepted it like it was the most natural thing in the world to do. I guess a good cry can do that. I knew it could, but to see it demonstrated so dramatically was a little startling.

Too dark to do much except just try to keep as warm as possible for the night, he said. In the morning I'll find my way out of here without your help, okay?

Okay, I said, as cheerfully as I could. I suddenly realized that if I kept to my goal, if I kept him out here, he might very well do damage to himself, up to and including getting himself killed from the cold.

As he began pacing around the area, looking for a nook to crawl into, I guess, both our spines tingled and our bodies got noticeably colder. Wet heavy drops of rain spattered on our heads. I groaned. It can't be raining, I said.

Quit being a complainer, he said. Help me find something to keep the rain off of us.

He reached up for some branches of a tree and I helped him snap the branches off. They had some needles on them, soft and wide.

We'll spread them over us, he said. If we get enough of them, they'll keep the rain off us. Off me, anyway. I don't think I care about you.

Hey! I said. I care about you.

Do not. You just want me to die.

No! I want you to be self-sufficient.

I'm a kid, he said. I don't know how to be that. You're grown up. You're supposed to watch out for me, not the other way around.

How do you know so much? I said.

There's nothing to know, he said. That's just the way life is. Didn't anyone ever tell you?

No one told me. Is it in the book?

That stopped him. He didn't have an answer for that. We snapped off more branches and he stuck them into the ground in a circle, so that all the fronds met in the center of the circle and made a kind of primitive dome there in the forest. It was getting harder and harder to see anything, but it looked like it might actually do what it was supposed to do. We got more branches, lots of them, and added to the circle. He was wet, but he didn't care. He should have cared. If you get too wet and cold you could be in trouble, but the rain was not as bad as those first few drops would have made you believe. Most of the rain was just mist, really. A dampness in the air.

When we finished, two dozen branches looked like they had sprouted out of the ground in a circle and joined green hands at the top. The kid crawled inside the dome and dragged me with him. I flowed through the fronds, greenery scraping by me like a net, and we both hunkered down with our heads kind of hanging and our legs folded up under us.

This going to work? I said. I was doubtful it had the integrity to withstand a night in the woods, especially a wet night. He didn't answer my question.

How do you know about the book? he said.

I know everything about you. I am you. Or was you. Something.

You aren't, he said. If you were me, then you'd be here.

He touched his forehead.

There are mysteries, kid, I said. There are things you don't understand. Things no one understands.

He put his hands over his head. Drops began to pelt the dome with increased strength and regularity. So far we were staying dry, although the ground itself, where we sat, was wet.

I don't know if I can stay out here all night, he said.

I didn't know either. We were going to be hungry pretty soon. And thirsty. I sought to distract him from his troubles.

You know there isn't any such book, right, kid?

He ran his sleeve over his nose, collecting a trail of snot on it. Disgusting.

Can't you use some leaves or something? I said.

Again, he didn't answer. He was good at ignoring me.

What are you going to do when you have to pee? I said. Or shit? Have you thought about that? You'll have to go outside.

I know that, he said.

How? I said.

What do you mean?

How do you know? Did you read the book?

No! he said, loudly and with some vehemence. I haven't read the book. I've never seen the book.

But, I pointed out to him, you still know stuff. How do you know stuff without the book? Have you ever wondered that?

I don't know the real important things, he said.

Are you alive?

What? he said.

Answer me. Are you alive?

Well, yeah. What a stupid question.

I ignored his impertinence. Okay, I said, you're alive. And have been for some time. Are you healthy?

He hesitated a long time, but eventually answered. Yeah, I'm healthy.

You're alive and healthy, and you have a place to live and you have parents who love you. You figured out how to get all that without the book. You must be some kind of genius!

I'm not a genius, he said.

Oh. Then how did you get the knowledge to do your school work and collect tadpoles and climb around in the tangle? How did you acquire all that knowledge without being a genius and without the book?

Born with it? he asked.

I let his question hang in the air. Splatters of rain were now pelting the dome, but hardly anything filtered down to us.

This shelter, I said. How did you know how to build it? Read it in the book?

He shook his head. Just figured it out. You stand under a tree, you'll stay dry. I figured it must be the needles. So I made this place for us. For me.

You can say us, kid, I said.

I really don't want to, he said.

Suit yourself, I told him. But we're not that different you know. You and me.

He pushed some leaves into a pile with his hands and his feet. I made a motion to help him, then remembered I could not. He worked methodically, gathering heaps of leaves into one big mound. Then he leaned over and curled up into a snail's position, turning in on himself. He brought his knees up to his chest and he wrapped his arms around his calves. I saw where I used to be him, how we fit together, congruent, but there was something, small details, that I saw already wouldn't quite work. I was already growing bigger than him. My outer confines could not be held within his frame.

Instead, I molded myself to the interior of the dome, letting my being snake around the curve and attach itself there, like I was some kind of adhesive tape stuck on the wall. I was still attached to the kid. Right at the ankle. I twisted around to look at the point where we were joined. I couldn't see anything out of the ordinary, no lock and chain, no wire, no nails, spikes, or staples. No rope, no twine, no glue. Nothing. Just his ankle and my ankle and nothing separating them. I put my hand in the wedge where they joined. I felt around for some way to sever the connection, but none came to me. I wondered if we were to be joined like this for eternity. I was not at all sure I could tolerate that. I was getting bigger, for one thing. My body, unconfined by matter's random boundaries, had found the wide open spaces particularly alluring. If I could not travel to distant realms, I would expand into them. It seemed reasonable. Even now, looking back on that peculiar night, I recall the feeling I had that nothing could keep me from the distant horizons, mysterious as they were. I never again had the experience of believing it was reasonable to think that I might encompass the entirety of the universe.

My career in mathematics gave me the ability to imagine such things: infinity and its manifestations are the stuff of mathematical inquiry and mathematical game playing, after all. We toss around those concepts with the flick of a symbol, somehow thinking we are playing with the forces of the universe when all we are doing is shuffling around marks on a page according to some esoteric rules we have made up. It sometimes pains me to think that I spent my productive middle years doing such things. I was reaching for something, for some ultimate meaning and purpose, and I had thought it would be in those mathematical concepts that I had some inkling of on that rainy night under the dome. Can you imagine the thoughts that ran through me in the darkness then? That my consciousness might expand so that the Earth could be a distant dot in the center. Less than a dot. The merest hint of something, lost way in the past. And that stars, even galaxies of stars, might be mere islands of fire embedded in my all-encompassing sweep of volume. The edges of me would be the edges of the universe. I craved the possibility of it. A few nights earlier, as the kid, I had thought to try to count to one million in my head. I started and got to not more than six hundred and fifty before falling asleep. The next day I calculated that it would take many many days of counting to get to one million. I thought it was possible, but not worth the time, so I gave up the attempt. This thought of growing as big as the universe had that same aspect to my mind. I thought it was possible. And what's more, I thought it was worth my time. And yet, here I was, still locked to the kid's ankle. I suppose many people have moments in their lives that define them. And I suppose many people return to that moment again and again throughout their lives, to savor it or, perhaps, to try to relive it. Bringing it back to them. It's like lost love, the need to bring that experience back. Once you have love, you don't ever want to be without it. Those few hours under the makeshift dome are my touchstone for all the subsequent days of my life. It was the time that I thought my life in Valton might be only a prelude to the great wide world awaiting me.

Such thoughts. Such concepts. I had no idea.

The boy had not been in stasis while I was musing about the universe. I came out of my extended thoughts of the world to find him sleep breathing. I thought to try to pull away from him then, reasoning that perhaps the unconsciousness of sleep might cause his grip to loosen, but it did not. We were still held as tightly as before. I felt the dome on my back and the leaves under me and his sleeping, so attuned with my own being, lulled me into a somnolent state. I didn't know where my weariness came from, but it soon overwhelmed me, and I slipped off to sleep of my own, during which I did not dream. I felt like only an instant had passed, but as I opened my eyes and surveyed my surroundings, found morning light streaming in through the tiny gaps in the fronds above me. They cast a strange light on the ground, little dots of illumination, like a patchwork quilt of them laying over the ground. They didn't lay on me, of course, but went right through me, as though I wasn't there. It took me a second to realize the kid wasn't there either. He had obviously exited the dome and left me alone.

I hardly even thought about the fact that we had severed our tie. I was now free of him, which was exactly what I had wanted with a fevered passion only a few hours before. But now? In the morning, with the cool air of a new day beginning to swirl around me, the expansive space of it larger than seemed reasonable, I found that I needed the familiarity of the kid's connection. I sought to desire the great circle of being, the wide world beyond, but I was loose in that wide world. I had no anchor. Without a defining and stable foundation, I wanted only the familiar. It was a complete surprise to me.

I pushed myself up from the floor of the dome and through the fronds. The rain from the previous evening had left the dome and the surrounding grounds damp. I did not feel the chill, however, since I was spirit, not mass. Or something. I wasn't sure what I was. I assumed I was some kind of ghost, born of trauma, but that was only a working hypothesis. Since that morning I have wondered what happened to me then. I have read accounts of spirits by many writers, some I thought had things to say, others who were simply deluded or crackpots. I have looked into spiritual matters, investigated religions, read numerous accounts of traumatic incidents, and in all cases I have not discovered an explanation for my particular circumstance. Not that I think of myself as exceptional, but surely I was not unique? I realize, of course, that one incident does not make a theory, but how else to view the events? How to think of myself, as I was then, has troubled me and occupied my mind ever since.

But let me continue the narrative. I pulled myself up and looked around the dome. The trees seemed less menacing than the previous night. Everything was bright. Almost overpoweringly so, as if the world wanted to imprint its cheerfulness on me despite my doubts about the world and its arrangements. I was not a nine year old boy anymore, but I still had a nine year old's spirit, and perhaps that amounts to the same thing. I moved over the ground with a locomotive impulse akin to walking, yet different from it. I would not exactly call it floating, but it had a certain congruence with that sensation. My feet dragged along the forest floor, moving through ferns and dried leaves like I was a mouse flitting in and out of debris. A breeze, gentle but insistent, moved through me, a cousin of my being at that moment, and yet indelibly different, as though two incompatible manifestations of the breath of the earth had coalesced into a warring confrontation over my being. I thought of the wind as something I could be. Or had been. Or would become.

It was tempting, in those first few moments, to fall under the spell of the wind. I recognized in its restless meanderings a congruence with my own urge to roam. My spirit had a need, which I mentioned earlier, that wanted to be bigger than it was. That's exactly what I felt in the wind as it blew through my being. It wanted to be bigger, always pushing itself beyond the boundaries set by atmospheric pressure and the physics of air movement over land and through trees.

It was not exactly that I wanted to take in the wind and add it to my insubstantial form, but more the feeling that the wind and I were cut from the same original billowing expanse of air. Or ether. An old fashioned term, I know, but from my current perspective it is the word that most captures the feeling I had.

I let the wind course through me for several minutes. It was, I think, the most at home I felt in my new incarnation, and it was not destined to last. How could it? I was a restless spirit, after all. If I didn't reunite with the kid, what was I going to be? How was I to be in the world?

Presently, as the sun rose higher above the horizon, and its warm rays streamed through me, I began to understand myself in more prosaic terms. I was not, after all, some exalted manifestation of spirit. I was, instead, more like a misplaced thought.

Yes, my perceptions of the world and my place in it were mercurial to the extreme. I flitted about like a leaf in the wind. I could not help it. I grasped for some anchor when I saw that

I was so insubstantial that light went through me. Light, which could be stopped by the thinnest slip of paper, managed to penetrate me with no difficulty at all. That observation sobered me immensely. I wanted to grab up some of that light and feed my soul with it. In fact, I made the attempt, twisting my will into a grasping posture. My memory of muscle movement and muscle strength gave me something of a blueprint for how to proceed as I bent my body this way and twisted it that, but nothing I did allowed me to wrap myself around any of that light. It was as though I was trying to consume an idea. I felt it, there, warming my being, but I could not then extend my reach any further and the light remained a distant grail. So far away that it might as well have been in another galaxy.

I remembered, when I had been part of the kid, times with a magnifying glass, when, on hot days, we would angle the rays through the lens and focus the resulting little circle of heat onto a piece of wood and watch smoke curl up from it. My friend sometimes used the lens to scorch bugs. Once made a caterpillar writhe under its needle sharp light dagger. This fascinated and repulsed me. I did not know if I liked him more or less after he caused the caterpillar such distress, but we remained friends nonetheless. I do think I felt some kind of respect for him. He had the temerity to harness the power of light to cause damage to a living creature. My response to this was complex, involving a loathing for the act, and an admiration for the mechanism. I hesitate to ascribe anything named evil to one so young, but perhaps that admiration for wickedness is the genesis of something that might be called evil in the future? A tough call. I didn't want to admire my friend's cruelty, and yet I could not help the feeling that his actions were some kind of admirable strength.

I can even, now, see that my friend was merely behaving in a typically inept and clumsy fashion. He was being a nine year old himself, trying to understand the world, trying out his power in a way that did him no respect, but that did not necessarily negate him as an individual. We should all be forgiven for the actions we took before, say, age fifteen or so. Maybe sixteen. And then, we should still be forgiven some of our transgressions. Others we would need to be held accountable for. The particular division of those acts would surely be something that might be debated for all eternity. In fact, I think they have. But for a kid at that age, taking in the world and attempting to understand his place in it, all acts have the same moral standing.

Up to a point. I ran from the boy I kicked not because I wanted an adventure in the woods, but because I sensed I had done something I shouldn't have. The bully was wrong, but so was I wrong in my retaliation. The fact that I had been attacked first did not excuse my behavior. It was difficult to understand that, and the difficulty sent me running. And ultimately split me.

And now here I was. A disembodied something floating in the world.

It took me a while to understand that I needed to reunite

with the kid. I didn't want the great vast universe after all. I just wanted to come home.

We had separated in the night. Or maybe early morning. Now I was alone. Let me turn to the outside world, as my internal musings are getting me nowhere fast. The leaves at my feet didn't crunch. How could they, since I was not material existence? I stepped forward. I moved forward. The sky over my head seemed real enough. I liked the blue. And the clouds accenting it were also deeply white. I had this notion of the clouds as the skeleton of the sky. It gave me comfort to think in those terms. A ridiculous conceit. I knew it even then. But I hung onto it. Like it explained something to me. Like I was the spiritual skeleton of the kid. I, in my substantial insubstantial way, existed to prop up the kid. By being separated from him, I was not fulfilling my purpose.

The thought chilled me. I felt a shiver of recognition ignite my being. It was similar to a feeling I would have years later when I first encountered Cantor's proof that infinity comes in various sizes. That realization hit me with an impact which moved me in my life's direction, which has been to explore the intricacies of mathematical experience. Never mind that the quest eventually lost its lustre. For a while it was there. The sudden gob-smack of perception, the opening of the world to a new point of view.

I had it, then. The sky tilted and slid away from me. A vertiginous feeling of helplessness gripped me and I found that I had lost my balance, not through lack of observation or carelessness, not by being distracted, no. None of these things. I lost my balance because I had begun to sink into the ground.

I looked down and saw that the leaves covering the floor of the forest were at the level of my calves. I dragged my feet through the earth and encountered the lines of roots and the grit of dirt and the sliminess of worms and bugs. Little pinpricks of unsprouted seeds scratched at me. The ground, in all its glorious bounty, seemed to want to interact with me and I felt nothing but irritation for it.

I was sinking? Into the ground?

Now why didn't anyone tell me about that? It seemed that I was more than nothing. I had some mass. Sufficient, at least, for gravity to wedge its jaws into me and pull me down.

I was able to drag my legs through the muck, but the tangle there would not release me. It was as though I had plunged my feet into a vat of roiling snakes and the snakes were only too happy to wrap themselves around me. Indeed, they behaved rather like ghostly snakes, because all that conflation of elements in the ground coalesced into an all enfolding, all encompassing embrace of my spirit.

If I were, now, as an old man, presented with something so counter to my life's experience, I think that I might faint dead away, such is my comfort with the way things are. Back then, much of life was still new and when presented with novel experiences, I was able to assimilate them into my world view. So it was that I was not overly distressed to learn that ghosts were not the floaty things that we had all been led to believe in. They were, in fact, a vital part of the real world. So I didn't panic. Didn't rage against the fates. Did not, in fact, feel it even peculiar after the first few seconds. It seemed, on the face of it, perfectly reasonable to think that the earth might want to pull my spirit self into itself. After all, we are all, ultimately, made from the stuff of the earth. We all want to go home and home has a pull on us, as if home wants us to come back. Anyone of a certain age will understand what I am saying.

The only thing that bothered me was that I might not be reunited with the kid.

I took more steps. Waded through the earth like someone stepping through a pool, pushing aside the water like it was made of something that came from the primordial depths.

Which, I suppose, it had.

Before long I had sunk to knee height. I still walked, but it was slower.

That's when I heard the explosion.

I think I felt it first. A slight trembling in the earth. Where it gripped my legs, I experienced a shaking like what might transpire in an earthquake. But then the sound. Like a flower blooming in super fast motion. A blemish in the world expanded all around me. I turned to try to see the source. It came from the mine. Suddenly I thought of miners trapped under the surface. Their screams as the walls of rock around them collapsed. The agony as the weight of those rocks crushed them.

But there were no screams. I saw the shafts, two silos on the horizon, but they looked undisturbed. No smoke wafted from them. No troubling crack presented itself on their facades. All looked calm and normal. Which suddenly felt completely abnormal.

The explosion, whatever it was, had also bumped me further into the ground. I was now buried up to my waist. Moving was getting even slower. My feet encountered denser soil. Clay-like in its weight and compact mass. It was as though I had run into a block of ice in the pool.

And then another shake. The world adjusting itself? Who knew? That's what it felt like, but my perspective was so limited. I could not see the big picture. Especially as it made me slip even further into the ground. Up to my arm pits. I lifted my arms, to try to keep them above the surface. The leaves were at my chin. The ferns now towered over me. My feet, impossibly far down, encountered rock, as any journey in this part of the country would do eventually. The soil of Valton and environs existed on top of a vast expanse of rock. It permeated the land and the souls of the people who lived there. Even I, a boy, knew that much. Knew the people here had to be hard to survive the harsh land.

I wanted to stand on that rock, four feet below me, but I did not. I slipped further and before long was up to my nose. Now my eyes were less than an inch above the leaves. I saw the veins in them, brown and deteriorated, but still evident, and wept for the beauty of nature. Then I lifted my arms and flailed at the sky, trying to grab hold of something, whether it was a cloud, a branch, a rock, or a twig. Anything to hold me up.

I heard voices behind me. Men in a group at the dome. Excited voices. Evidently a search party looking for the kid. They had found evidence of his encampment. How long had they been searching? All night? Or did they just begin this morning?

I had no time to see who they were or what they were doing. The earth shook again.

The boots. The boots of the searchers. That was the explosion I had heard earlier. Their stomps and footfalls was enough to shake me into the ground. As they walked by me, the earth shook and trembled even more. It made tiny pockets of motion and I slipped into those pockets. Even further. Before long I was completely under the surface, immersed in the brown-black expanse of soil.

And now here the wisdom of nature asserted itself in a most disconcerting way. I knew in a way I could not explain, where to find the kid.

I oriented myself in a southerly direction—here is another miracle: I knew how to orient myself according to the poles of the earth—and began swimming through the earth. I found I was able to ride up high, in the less dense soil that supported the trees and was being constantly managed by the worms, turning over granules and adding their bit to the enterprise. I used a crawl stroke because it seemed most natural. I wind-milled my arms and kicked my legs. I propelled myself so well that within a few moments I felt like I had been born to the activity. Occasionally I pushed myself up and burst through the surface to look around, but found that I felt comfortable underground and retreated to its entanglements and cozy proximity. All the granules pressed themselves against my being in a conglomeration of sensation. Not unlike the feeling of dipping one's hand in a bowl of marbles.

I sensed the cemetery before I got to it. The ground had been tampered with up ahead. I could tell by the tendrils of energy emanating from it and intersecting my being as I swam. Before I arrived at any coffins, I paused.

I hovered in the ground, treading dirt, as it were, bracing myself for my return to the kid. I pushed myself up and burst through the surface. I was on a grassy stretch of greenery. Tombstones loomed ten feet away. I expected to see the kid in front of his sister's stone, but I was disappointed to see the cemetery was empty. My guess had been wrong? It seemed hardly possible. The urge to come here was so strong. It had to mean something. I pushed myself over to our sister's gravesite. I saw footprints. Fresh ones in the wet grass and muddy soil.

He had been here. I was not far wrong. So now where did he go?

I followed the tracks. They led away from the cemetery, and ended at the edge of the road that went from Valton to the mine. The road that all the miners used to get to work.

I swam across the road. The asphalt felt scratchy, like someone dragging their nails over my skin. I didn't find any tracks on the other side.

So.

Evidently the kid was walking on the road? I looked north toward the mine. The road curved and disappeared around a stand of tall trees. I looked south. A few houses, the edge of Valton, sat a half mile or so away. The town was that way, but something more important than the town also beckoned.

I dove back into the ground and churned my way through the soil with rapidity and grace. I was good at this. Before long I came to the very east edge of Valton. Where the bull dozers had piled up all the trees that used to stand where Valton now stood.

I dove under the tangle and came up from its bottom. I burst through the surface and immediately lifted my head to the crisscross entanglement of all those trees, piled up into a kind of entwining rabble. Mice ran through me, excitedly. Were they able to perceive me, or was it just coincidence that I stood in their paths? No way to tell. I put my hands on the ground and pushed myself up even further. My head pushed through a nest made of leaves and twigs. Raccoon? Couldn't tell. In any case, it was abandoned.

Diffuse light sifted in from the top of the tangle, which seemed impossibly high over my head. I used the dead trees to pull me up. Evidently I had learned something while swimming through the ground. I was able to interact enough with the world to help me navigate this space. I sat on a log and put my palm on the face of a shelf fungus which had grown to impressive proportions here.

I sat. Took in my surroundings. The darkness was like a palpable thing. I felt like I could cut it, the way I might cut a cake. I liked it. After the darkness of the ground, it seemed completely welcoming and benign.

I'm not sure how long I was there. Maybe five seconds. Maybe five minutes. Time had a different texture. It was as though all of existence had conspired in that moment to give me solace, and so I took it.

Gradually I heard voices. Not the voices of men, not like the ones who were looking for the kid. Looking for me, but the voices of children. Boys. They came from above me in the tangle. I climbed up through the tangle, limbs touching trees like a spider climbing her web. As I moved I tried to discern the voices. Three of them. They were talking easily, as though they were friends, but something in me knew they were not friends. At least, not completely. There was something else between them that resisted the understanding that comes with true friendship.

The first voice was easy. It was my friend's voice. The one that I had been hunting tadpoles with. The second was more difficult, until I realized it was the rock thrower. And the third was hardest of all. It had a familiar quality, but it took me an embarrassingly long time to realize that I had heard the voice often, only from a different perspective. More internal.

The third voice was my own.

And all these three, this unlikely tribe of kids, were talking quietly. Almost reverently in the tangle.

The tangle invited such an attitude. There was a quality of space in the jutting and crossed trees that suggested a still forest.

Anyway, said the voice that was mine, thanks for the food.

It's okay, said the rock thrower. I'm sorry I did that to you. Gave you a cut.

It's no big deal.

I moved closer to the trio. They had this quality of camaraderie which I found wholly unnerving and foreign.

I saw they were all eating sandwiches and picking chips from bags and munching on them. A backpack lay next to them.

I didn't bleed to death or nothing, said my voice.

The rock thrower laughed. You guys looked so stupid down there, I just had to throw rocks.

My friend nodded. And you looked so stupid on the tracks, I wanted you to die.

Then all three laughed and then they fell silent and went back to eating their sandwiches.

I'm okay, my voice said, but I'm going to catch hell when my parents find me.

The other two boys nodded.

I had to come here, though. After my sister.

That's rough about your sister, said the rock thrower.

Yeah, I said. That rock you threw, it didn't kill me or anything, but it did something to me. I feel different now, you know. Like something fell out of me.

The other two stopped chewing. They felt the strange tone in my words. I felt it too. I moved closer to the kid. There was a magnetic pull between us. I don't know if he felt it, but I did. I couldn't pull away. It was like attracting like, I suppose, which went counter to the normal course of events.

He kept talking, speaking for both us, though he didn't know it.

I lost the world, I said. I don't know how else to explain it. When that rock hit me, it was like everything I had ever thought about the world was different. All of it disappeared and I was empty. Nothing inside of me. I ran into the woods and made a shelter. I wanted to be there. I wanted to feel the forest.

He looked down at the tangle of trees.

So now here I am, he said. I'm in what used to be a forest, but I'm still empty. I still don't feel right.

I put out my foot, so it contacted his foot. He twitched. Almost fell off his perch. The other two grabbed his shoulders and steadied him.

Then we merged back into one. It was a quick zipping process, like bringing the halves of a plastic bag together to seal the top.

I blinked. I shrugged my shoulders to get the muscles to sit right on my being. I wiggled my arms to fit myself perfectly into the skeleton and muscles and joints. Everything felt exactly right.

Then our voices and our thoughts came together.

I wanted to kill you, I said. But then when I saw my sister's grave, everything was different. I didn't want to kill anything.

The rock thrower looked me in the eyes. It was like he was searching for a speck of something lost.

You just shifted, he said, a hint of suspicion in his voice.

My friend, the one who wouldn't help me save the rock thrower's life, began weeping. I was embarrassed for him. I wanted him to stop.

I thought you were both going to die, he said between sobs, and I didn't know what to do. I was frozen. I felt like I was such a sissy.

And here I think was the first time that I saw another human being for something other than what my eyes presented to me. I felt as though I had the power to penetrate his very essence. In a rotting pile of trees on the edge of a squalid little mining town, my world not only expanded in those few seconds, but it also made me feel the power of comprehension.

We're all sissies, I said. Everyone is.

They looked at me and waited, like they wanted to hear what I was going to say next.

Sometimes, I continued, we can hide it better than other times.

About the Author

Mario Milosevic's novels include *Claypot Dreamstance, The Coma Monologues, The Last Giant,* and *Kyle's War.* His poetry collections include *Fantasy Life* and *Animal Life.* He lives and writes in the Pacific Northwest of the United States. Learn more at mariowrites.com.